"Are you a good pilot?"

Sarah could have kicked herself. That had sounded so rude and was a pretty stupid question at that. What did she expect him to say? *"No, I crash once a week."*

Kip laughed. "I'm told I am. Everyone's always landed in the same general condition they boarded in. That help?"

She noticed his grin was a little crooked but kind. "Not really," she replied truthfully and felt a blush stain her cheeks.

She held the armrest in a white-knuckled grip as he flipped a bunch of switches, and the plane's propellers started to spin. He patted her hand. "Just sit back and try to relax. I'm not going to let anything happen to you or baby Grace. You're both safe with me."

His smile was once again reassuring. So reassuring she had a hard time looking away. And for the first time since her principal and two National Guard officers knocked on her classroom door to give her the bad news about Scott, Sarah didn't feel alone. It was ridiculous but Kip Webster m.......
even.

Books by Kate Welsh

Love Inspired

*For the Sake of
   Her Child* #39
Never Lie to an Angel #69
A Family for Christmas #83
Small-Town Dreams #100
Their Forever Love #120
*The Girl Next Door #156
*Silver Lining #173
*Mountain Laurel #187

*Her Perfect Match #196
Home to Safe Harbor #213
*A Love Beyond #218
*Abiding Love #252
*Autumn Promises #265
Redeeming Travis #271
Joy in His Heart #325
Time for Grace #446

*Laurel Glen

KATE WELSH

is a two-time winner of Romance Writers of America's coveted Golden Heart Award and a finalist for RWA's RITA® Award in 1999. Kate lives in Havertown, Pennsylvania, with her husband of over thirty years. When not at work in her home office, creating stories and the characters that populate them, Kate fills her time in other creative outlets. There are few crafts she hasn't tried at least once or a sewing project that hasn't been a delicious temptation. Those ideas she can't resist grace her home or those of friends and family.

As a child she often lost herself in creating make-believe worlds and happily-ever-after tales. Kate turned back to creating happy endings when her husband challenged her to write down the stories in her head. With Jesus so much a part of her life, Kate found it natural to incorporate Him in her writing. Her goal is to entertain her readers with wholesome stories of the love between two people the Lord has brought together and to teach His truths while she entertains.

Time for Grace
Kate Welsh

Steeple
Hill®

Published by Steeple Hill Books™

STEEPLE HILL BOOKS

Steeple
Hill®

ISBN-13: 978-0-373-81360-5
ISBN-10:   0-373-81360-0

TIME FOR GRACE

Are not two sparrows sold for a farthing? And one of them shall not fall on the ground without your Father. But the very hairs of your head are all numbered. Fear ye not therefore, ye are of more value than many sparrows.

—Matthew 10:29–31

For Jane, who never gave up hope and against all odds fought valiantly for her child. And for Kelly, the little miracle whose fighting spirit confounded the experts and taught us all that anything is possible. May your futures be bright with promise.

Chapter One

Sarah trailed behind Grace's travel Isolette with its built-in ventilator. The ambulance attendants and neonatal nurses kept a careful watch over Grace as they moved toward the blue-and-white plane that stood waiting for them. The pilot, his golden hair blowing in the stiff November breeze, wore what looked like a World War II flight jacket. It looked as if he was checking the little blue plane from a list on a clipboard.

Sarah shivered. Little planes. She'd hated them from the first plane ride she could remember at age four. She and her parents had flown to a small settlement in Africa, landing on a bumpy rutted strip of dirt that she still thought must have rattled her baby teeth loose.

The logo on the blue plane was made up of what appeared to be angel's wings that were attached to a cloud. Agape Air was written in a semicircle below. Once, in the past, her worry would have eased at the thought of the word *agape*. It was the kind of love she'd been taught came from God alone. These days Sarah had a hard time believing He loved her at all.

That He cared at all.

He'd let Scott die, hadn't He? And with him the promise of a better, happier life.

He'd let their precious baby enter the world too soon. Now Grace's every breath was a struggle to stay alive.

And as far back as the very beginnings of Sarah's life, He'd sent her to parents so busy doing His bidding that she'd always been an afterthought. Her disappointment in them was such an old and uncomfortable wound she wondered why she kept revisiting it time and again. It was futile and painful. Sort of like poking a sore tooth with her tongue.

The thing was, she missed her parents and not Scott at times like this, just as she'd missed them in nearly every moment of doubt and pain all through her life.

Maybe that was because she and Scott had

had so little time together. They'd met at work and dated during the second half of a busy school year. She'd joined the Piedmont Point Christian School's staff in January after leaving her post at an African mission in Doctal. Scott had started talking about the possibility of marriage not all that long after they met. And then, within a month of those preliminary chats about a possible future, his National Guard unit had been called up. He'd gotten a little frantic, not wanting to leave for war again without the bond of marriage between them. So even though she'd had doubts, felt rushed and as if something was missing between them, Sarah hadn't had the heart to say no.

He'd left for Iraq a bit over a week after their small hurried wedding. And then, within three weeks, Scott was gone forever. All they'd had as man and wife was a one-week honeymoon and the two exhausting days before he left that they'd used to move his things into her apartment.

Sarah hadn't yet come to depend on him. She hadn't had a chance to get used to his day-in and day-out company and emotional support.

She knew what she missed about Scott

were all those possibilities they'd talked about.

The hopes.

The dreams.

The plans that had never had a chance to come to fruition. Togetherness. Belonging. A happy, devoted family life. All the things she'd always wanted so desperately but had been denied.

And had been denied again.

The truth was that Scott couldn't help being dead. And she was confident that he was happy in heaven. But she was still here and alone while her parents were, once again, off serving God, too busy to offer comfort to their only child.

Sarah knew she was always mentioned in her parents' prayers, but she'd wanted them at her wedding. She'd wanted their arms around her at Scott's funeral. She'd wanted them to fly to her side when her child was born so early and so fragile. This past Thursday she'd wanted what her friends from college and the school where she worked had had. She'd wanted a family, a turkey and her child strong and healthy.

She shook her head. When would she learn? Unfair as it felt, to her parents as

God's soldiers in a war for souls, she was, and always had been, insignificant.

So she'd spent the holiday alone at the hospital, trying to bond with a baby she couldn't even hold. And worrying because Grace still hadn't gained even an ounce over her birth weight since her birth six weeks earlier.

Instantly Sarah felt selfish and guilty the way only her jealousy over her parents' other commitments could make her feel. Their work was important. She knew that. But couldn't she come first with them just once? Just for a little while?

This past Thanksgiving weekend was supposed to have been about family and giving thanks for all the blessings life held. Sarah had had a hard time thanking God when her parents were in a far-off land, her husband was dead and their baby barely clung to life.

She tried to remember that it was a friend of her parents', Doctor Joachim Prentice, who'd agreed to evaluate Grace and if possible operate, and that they'd offered to pay for the surgery. And that through their contacts, they'd secured the help of Angel Flight East. Angel Flight was a volunteer organization of pilots and plane owners. They flew critically ill patients and their family members—like Grace and herself—free of charge in their personal aircraft to hospitals for treatment. She would be forever grateful for the organization and the small airline who'd loaned their plane for the trip.

Sarah glanced ahead at the tiny plane that was to take them to Philadelphia. It didn't look any bigger now that she'd gotten closer to it. Out of habit she found herself praying that God would watch over the plane and Grace during the flight. Her child had defied the odds so far but now her heart—the heart that had astounded the doctors at her birth by continuing to beat in her one-pound-three-ounce body—was in trouble.

"Mrs. Bates," a deep voice said, breaking into her thoughts.

Sarah turned toward the voice, realizing she'd reached the plane. The blazing sun was so blinding this close to the shining blue-and-white fuselage that she could see only the man's tall, imposing outline. "Oh, am I in the way of you and your checklist?"

He shook his head. "No. You aren't in my way at all."

Sarah blinked, trying not to stare as the

pilot stepped into the shadow of the plane. She blinked again. Except that his hair was a few shades lighter, he looked like a very young Jimmy Stewart as she'd seen him in an old movie. His vintage flight jacket and wire-framed aviator sunglasses only helped the World War II reference along.

"I wanted to welcome you aboard," the pilot continued, "and offer you the copilot seat for the flight. There's not a lot of comfortable seating in the rear. I had to take out two seats for that whizbang Isolette I brought along from Children's Hospital. That only left the two for your baby's nurses and a bench that's hard as a rock. You'd be a lot more comfortable up front. Suppose we go check on Grace, then we'll get this show on the road?"

Sarah nodded, impressed that he'd cared enough to learn her baby's first name. So many of the doctors and nurses referred to Grace as the Bates baby. She'd heard that somewhere in history children weren't named till their first birthday because infant mortality rates had been so high. But she'd given her baby a name. And Sarah wanted her to live. She'd move mountains to make sure Grace had every chance.

The pilot climbed the steps into the plane then stood aside while Sarah entered the small fuselage. Once again she had to give him credit. When they reached Grace's Isolette, he didn't recoil or gasp at the sight of her tiny daughter as her fellow teachers at Piedmont Point had. Grace's pale skin was still nearly translucent, her musculature and blood vessels still evident to the naked eye. Sarah herself had been shocked and frightened at her first close look at her child, wondering how her baby could survive.

When the pilot squatted down next to Grace's Isolette and took off his sunglasses, he proved he was made of sterner, kinder stuff than those others. He gave her daughter a sweet smile and tapped on the Plexiglas as if to gain Grace's attention.

"Hi there, sweetie," he said from his position on the floor. "I'll try for a real smooth ride for you. You just hang in there and we'll have you fixed up in no time."

Next he carefully checked the bracket, then tightened the strap that anchored the Isolette to the floor of the plane. When he stood, his deep green eyes were calm and steady. The expression seemed to promise that he was in control and he knew everything would be all right. She refused to believe anything else. Sarah would bring her child home one day. She just wasn't sure where home would be.

"I'm Kip Webster, your pilot today," he told the nurses and shook hands with each of them. "Do any of you have questions or concerns?"

Sarah had plenty but stayed silent. So did the nurses.

"Okay then, it looks like we're all set. Buckle up, ladies. Mrs. Bates, are you going to take the copilot seat?"

Sarah nodded. She'd sit where she'd be more comfortable but she had no intention of voicing any of the million questions she had about the flight or the plane. This man was part of a chain of people who had volunteered to try to save her child's life. She'd endure anything to make that happen. And that included sitting quietly in the cockpit of a tiny fly speck of a plane even if she had to hold her breath all the way to Philadelphia. She certainly didn't want to bother anyone with her fears.

Moments later she slid into the seat next to Kip and followed his instructions. Once buckled up, he handed her a pair of aviator sunglasses. "These are my extras," he said smiling again. "I noticed you squinting outside. The glare will only get worse once we're up. You'll have a monster headache halfway to Philly without them."

"Thanks. Are you a good pilot?" she asked and could have kicked herself. That had sounded so rude and was a pretty stupid question at that. What did she expect him to say? "No. I crash once a week!"

Kip Webster laughed. "I'm told I am. I've always managed to keep my planes in the air till it was time to land. And everyone's always landed in the same general condition they boarded in. That help?"

She grimaced. "Not really," she replied truthfully and felt a blush stain her cheeks.

She noticed his grin was a little crooked but kind. "Don't be embarrassed. Most people are skittish in small crafts the first time."

"But this isn't my first time. A lot of my flights have been in smaller planes. My parents are missionaries. I spent a good deal of my early life flying into makeshift airstrips in practically every back corner of the world."

She held the armrest in a white-knuckled

grip as he flipped a bunch of switches and the plane's propellers started to spin. He patted her hand. "Well, there you go. You're in for a treat today then. This field and the one on the other end are both smooth as glass. Just sit back and try to relax. I'm not going to let anything happen to you or Grace. You're both safe with me."

His smile was once again reassuring. So reassuring she had a hard time looking away. And for the first time since her principal and two National Guard officers knocked on her classroom door to give her the bad news about Scott, Sarah didn't feel alone. It was ridiculous but Kip Webster made her feel safe—protected even.

About ten minutes into the flight, Kip turned toward her. "Mrs. Bates, they told us Grace's daddy was killed in Iraq. You must feel terribly alone right now. But have faith. Dr. Prentice is the best. I fly kids to see him all the time. And I fly them home again when they're stronger and healthier. I wanted to express the condolences of everyone at Agape Air and Angel Flight East for your loss. My partner and I would be honored if you'd let us pick up your hotel tab while you're in the city."

She stared for a long moment. No empty platitudes had fallen from this man's mouth. Just that long quiet look, an honest expression of sympathy, then on to the living. She couldn't believe he'd offered to help by defraying some more of the cost of this trip for her.

"Thank you," she managed, startled not only at his generous offer but that he'd brought up Scott at all. Maybe because everyone she knew seemed to shy away from her when she tried to talk about him. Sarah was grateful to this man for yet another reason. Not only had he given up part of his holiday weekend for her daughter, he'd also given her the chance to talk about Scott.

He *had* lived. Their child was evidence of that. She found herself smiling. "His name was Scott. And please call me Sarah. He was killed in Baghdad by a roadside bomb. Enlisting in the Guard was his way of working through his anger over 9/11. He lost his older brother in the World Trade Center."

Kip winced. "I channeled my anger over the attacks by ferrying local firefighters back and forth from working up at Ground Zero and flying supplies to them. Scott's parents must be devastated to lose a second son. I can't imagine losing one of my nephews let alone two children of my own."

"Scott's parents were older when he was born and were both gone already when his brother died." She told him how briefly she and Scott had been married and ended by revealing something she'd felt from the moment she'd learned of her husband's death. "I think he knew he was going to die."

Kip nodded as if he somehow understood. "Was he was excited about the baby?"

She sighed. "I think that's my greatest regret. He never knew. But I'm still proud of him. Serving his country was what he thought was the right way to honor his older brother's memory."

Kip nodded and sort of tugged on the collar of his jacket. "This was my grandfather's. He flew B-29's in World War II. My dad was a fighter pilot in Vietnam. I thought about the Air Force but I had my pilot's license by the time I was seventeen. It felt like I'd be going backward in life since they wouldn't guarantee me flight school. I guess I got interested in the Angel Flight organization because it lets me volunteer to serve people in need and still do what I love."

"I'm certainly grateful for what you do.

And to your airline for lending the airplane. Grace couldn't have gotten to Philadelphia any other way."

Kip was always uncomfortable with gratitude from either the patients he was called on to ferry places for treatment or from their desperate family members. He did what he did in his free time to keep others from experiencing the pain of losing a loved one. His father's sudden death when Kip was only seven years old had shaped his life with a devastating kind of pain that he freely admitted he'd never gotten past. Nor had he been able to forget the sounds of his mother's grief as she'd cried into her pillow night after night. Probably because he'd cried silent tears right along with her.

When his father was followed in death by his uncle two years later everything got much worse. His aunt and his mother had pooled their resources to stay afloat. Raising eleven children under one roof in order to ease the financial burden that Kevin and Galen Webster left behind had made for one wild household full of women and girls—except for him.

Being the lone male hadn't always been

easy. But he loved women. He loved children. He'd wanted one day to be the kind of husband and father his had been all the while living in fear of losing his mother or aunt.

His fear changed and so did his plans for his future when his aunt sat him down days shy of his eighteenth birthday. She'd told him the truth about the Webster family affliction. Not a single Webster man in as many generations as had been recorded in the family bible had lived past the age of forty. She'd said their hearts were time bombs.

His heart.

And she'd said that the pain and grief could end with him because the heredity didn't seem to pass to the sons of Webster-born women. She'd urged him not to be as selfish as his uncle and father had been.

To let the grief end with him.

He'd remembered his mother at his father's funeral—that frozen look in her eyes. She'd looked so breakable and later that night in the privacy of her room he'd heard the shattering grief explode into tears.

He'd remembered the hollow look of his grandmother the days she'd buried each of her sons. He'd never known his granddad and that day he'd realized why. And worse, he'd known that his mom would one day stand at his grave, wearing that same hollow look of loss.

He'd remembered all mac-and-cheese dinners when he'd wished and prayed for a slice of meat. He hadn't complained though because it was his mom going off to work exhausted with awful colds and the remnants of stomach viruses that had paid for those meals.

Now he glanced at Sarah Bates. At her serviceable slacks and coat and her worn sneakers. Money was clearly tight for her just as it had been for his mom and aunt. Sarah was a pretty young woman with rich chestnut hair that she'd pulled back in a simple bouncing ponytail. Lively as her hair was whenever she moved her head, she wore a tired expression in her deep brown eyes that he'd seen too often in his mom's. Scott Bates's widow had more on her shoulders than she should have to bear alone.

And she was apparently very alone.

She reminded Kip why he lived his own life alone. No woman would ever struggle to overcome the burdens *he'd* left behind. No children would watch helpless to lend her their assistance. And no son of his would face the prospect of having only half a lifetime to do his living.

He'd tried to find out if there was anything wrong with his heart but his family doctor had shaken his head and told him he was imagining things. That he was healthy as a horse. Unfortunately, his aunt Emily had confided that his uncle Galen had passed a physical with flying colors the morning he died and his father, Kevin, had been an airline pilot with a clean bill of health, too. Every year Kip passed his flight physical and was deemed to be in good health but he knew that apparently it didn't mean a thing.

"So, how long do you think you'll be in Philly?" he asked Sarah, wanting to get his thoughts off himself.

"That's going to depend on what the doctor says. If he thinks he can fix Grace's heart problem, and he did seem to think he could, she'd be expected to stay till she can safely go back to Virginia." A look of concern creased the space between her eyebrows.

"Have you lived there all your life?"

She shook her head. "I've lived so many places it feels as if I've never lived anywhere. I thought Piedmont Point would be home. I have to be honest, though, I don't really want Grace to go back to Winston-Baily Medical Center. It's small and rural and I don't think it's the best place for her. When I went into labor so early, they acted as if she was already gone."

"They obviously changed their minds," he said and glanced back toward Grace.

Sarah smiled. "Because my daughter had other ideas. Each breath was a struggle for her, but she wouldn't give up, and that left them no choice. Even at one pound three ounces, Grace has twenty pounds of fight in her. She's going to make it."

Kip returned the grin that spoke of Sarah's parental pride in her tiny, plucky infant. "A force to be reckoned with, huh?"

She nodded, still wearing that soft, proud smile.

"I can see why you wouldn't want them responsible for her care but what will you do about your job? You're a teacher?"

Sarah nodded, her glossy, deep-brown ponytail bobbing at the back of her head. "At a K-through-twelve Christian school in Piedmont. I'm the school's art teacher. My maternity leave was over Friday but I can't just leave Grace in Philadelphia alone so…" She shrugged. "I just don't know. As I said, a lot depends on what Doctor Prentice says. And then, of course, how Grace does in surgery."

Kip looked away and pretended to check his instruments. He didn't even want to think of what would take Sarah back to West Virginia immediately. They both knew it would mean Grace wasn't a candidate for the surgery. And that would mean nothing could save her. There was also the very real possibility that the surgery itself could prove too much for Grace.

He prayed that neither would be the outcome for the valiant little girl who'd stolen his heart the moment he'd seen her little chest moving with each beat of her heart. Anyone that determined to survive deserved her shot at life. As always, Kip could only rely on faith and the Almighty's goodness and wisdom.

Lord, it's me again, Kip prayed silently. *I have another of Your little ones here with me. Please, bless every aspect of her trip. Bless Dr. Prentice with the skill to succeed. Bless Grace with the life she's so valiantly fighting to have.*

Kip looked next to him where Sarah Bates had turned to look back at her tiny baby—a look of hope and innocence shining from her deep brown eyes.

And, Lord, maybe You could send someone to watch out for Sarah, too.

Because much as he was tempted to lend a helping hand, Kip found Sarah Bates a little too special. And he always steered clear of temptation like that.

Chapter Two

Sarah woke groggily, conscious of being in her darkened hotel room near the hospital. As she pushed herself into a sitting position on the side of the bed, she thought of the University of Pennsylvania's Children's Hospital. It had been quite a surprise after Winston-Baily.

At CHOP, as everyone called the huge hospital, a bright happy lobby all dressed for the holidays had greeted her and Grace when they'd entered the huge facility. And that radiant, festive and nonthreatening atmosphere continued throughout.

A layer of Christmas cheer blanketed the entire facility. But she could tell the decorators hadn't sacrificed function or efficiency for ambiance. So far everyone and every procedure she'd witnessed had been methodical and professional. The staff were extremely serious about the health and well-being of the children in their care.

Many children there were older and stronger than Grace but just as many were fighting for life against cancer and varied severe birth defects. Grace's prospects suddenly seemed less tragic by comparison.

Unable to rest once her mind veered onto her child, Sarah jumped up, tore out her ponytail to run a comb through her hair and redo the simple practical style. She shrugged on her jacket, while already heading out her door and down the hall. As she dodged rush-hour traffic, she wondered if this big bustling city, that had been dressed up festively for the coming holiday, would become her new home or just another temporary stop in a life full of temporary stops.

After scrubbing up before entering the NICU, the hospital's Neo-natal Intensive Care Unit, Sarah looked around at the bright happy primary colors of the modern surfaces and equipment. Winston-Baily might have called their unit a NICU but this felt like a world, and not just a few states, away. She didn't need a medical degree to know Grace was better off here.

A nurse waved and motioned her toward the back of the nursery. At last Sarah entered and padded in, anxious to see Grace.

"Here she is, Mommy. All safe and sound," the same African-American nurse called out softly, motioning from the far end of the room.

Sarah hadn't met this nurse and could only imagine that something to do with the hospital's elaborate security system had let her know which baby Sarah belonged with. While walking back to Grace, she noticed that even the Isolettes were decorated with bows and Christmas balls. It was so nice to see all these tiny humans being treated like children who would notice their surroundings. That alone compelled her to take notice of the other babies.

Most were bigger than Grace and pinker with normal non-transparent skin. Many had less equipment attached to them and were clearly further along than Grace. But none were as beautiful or special. Not to Sarah anyway. But she wasn't so besotted with Grace that she didn't know their parents felt the same way about each and every one of them.

After looking her fill at Grace nestled in what had to be a state-of-the-art bed, Sarah looked up at the nurse. "Hi. I'm Sarah." She presented her identification bracelet for examination anyway. "How's she doing?"

The nurse checked the bracelet, compared it to one on Grace's thin ankle then smiled as she wrote something on the chart attached to her bed. "She settled right in. No surprises. That's what we hope for with a transfer."

"Why isn't she in an isolette?"

"This is what's called a flat bed. It makes handling her while she's still on the ventilator easier. The mattress keeps her warm so don't you worry. I'm Leslie Washington, Grace's evening nurse. Dr. Prentice was in a while ago. He asked me to have you stop in at his office when you got back."

Sarah nodded. "Can you give me directions? This place is enormous."

Nurse Washington nodded. "Sure is. Suppose I draw you a map to the doc's office so we don't lose you." She grabbed an eight-and-a-half by eleven form and flipped it over to the blank side and quickly sketched out a map to Dr. Prentice's office. After verbally explaining the directions, Leslie wrote the office number at the top. "I'll page him and have him meet you there. Good luck, honey."

After one more long look at Grace, Sarah started off for Doctor Prentice's office. It took nearly ten minutes but she found the doctor's suite exactly where Leslie said it would be. Sarah sank onto a comfy-looking sofa in the empty waiting room. She glanced through several parenting magazines and a few on fashion. Then she just closed her eyes and dropped her head back against the stiff leather upholstery and absorbed the feeling of knowing her baby was being well cared for.

"Sarah?" she heard from far away. "Sarah," called the voice again. She frowned, struggling to wake. She couldn't place the voice but she thought she'd heard it before. Curiosity helped her to force her eyes open. Standing before her was a tall, gray-haired man in a wacky Christmas-printed lab coat, a dress shirt and jeans. She might not have readily recognized his voice but his smile and his Disney print ties were unforgettable. Doctor Joachim Prentice.

"Dr. Prentice," she said, smiling back at him. They'd met in Africa when she'd joined her parents just after she'd graduated from

Liberty University with her teaching degree. He'd had such a striking rapport with the children in the refugee camp that he was impossible to forget. He'd jokingly claimed cartoon ties dissolved all social boundaries and language barriers. Sarah still thought it was his benevolent smile.

"I must have drifted off. Excuse me, please," she said, yawning as he backed up a few steps to lean against the receptionist's counter.

"Don't be silly. Sit. Sit," he ordered when she made a move to stand. "We can chat right here. We have the place to ourselves and my office is a mess anyway. And don't worry about the cat nap. It's understandable. I'm told you've been keeping quite a schedule at Winston-Baily."

"She does better when I'm around," she countered. "The nurses told me I was imagining it but I noticed a difference in Grace's oxygen levels when I'm with her."

"Actually, you're probably right but you're only human, Sarah. My first move with Grace will go a long way toward alleviating some of that stress on both of you. I'd like to start supplementing your milk with a special formula. It should help get some weight on her. And as important as bonding with her is, you can't spend all your time here. There's going to be plenty of time for you two after she goes home."

"I-I suppose," Sarah said, her mind whirling. He not only believed she was good for Grace, he believed she'd come home one day. Finally, here was someone with as much hope as she had. Her eyes filled with tears.

Doctor Prentice sat on the sofa next to her and handed her a tissue, then he covered her other hand with his. "Now don't start worrying about taking her home. You'll do fine when the time comes."

Sarah shook her head. He didn't get it. "It's not that. I can't wait to have Grace home with me no matter how much extra work she'll be. No one at Winston-Baily ever acted as if anything I did helped her, and none of them ever talked about her having a future. It was like I was the only one who believed she had one."

"Well, I don't see it that way," he said, sounding annoyed. "I looked her over a while ago and I studied her records before she got here. She looks better to me than they indicated and I was already pretty sure I'd be able to help her. I can see no reason not to do the surgery after we get her just a little stronger."

His phone rang and he answered it after checking the caller ID. Sarah felt profound disappointment and worry settle on her again. She'd thought the worry would be over by tomorrow. Now she'd be on pins and needles for weeks hoping against the odds that Grace would make it through surgery.

"That was Peter Kelly," Doctor Prentice explained after ending the call. "He's the neonatologist I called in on Grace's case. He'll take care of her everyday needs. You'll meet him a little later. He concurs that we should wait a couple weeks for the surgery."

Doctor Prentice pulled a small notebook out of his pocket then, and drew a diagram of a heart. "This isn't a rare problem Grace has," he said in a soothing tone. "Actually it's one of my more common surgeries," he told her, pointing to his drawing and explaining the surgery. He really made it sound routine.

That made Sarah feel better.

"Now on to the bonding problem. She'll have the same four nurses in twelve-hour rotations. We do this so they get to know her and she gets to know them. You really can't keep up a schedule of being with her all the time. Now let's talk about after her surgery."

Prentice sighed and raked his fingers through his already unkempt hair. "Sarah, I have to advise you not to take her back to Winston-Baily. I'm not trying to bad-mouth another facility, but here at CHOP we're used to kids like Grace. Those folks are simply out of their depth with a micro preemie. After surgery, we can transfer her to another children's hospital nearer there, if that would work better for you. I can make some calls."

It was almost a relief to hear her own thoughts confirmed. "No *place* is as important as Grace. I'm more than willing to move here for her sake. I'd been thinking about it already. I'll start trying to find a place to live and a teaching position right away."

He nodded. "That's good…that's fine. Grace has a couple tricky years ahead of her. She'll be better off here or I wouldn't suggest that you uproot yourself."

"If here is better for her, then here's where we'll be. West Virginia wasn't home anyway."

He glanced at his watch again. "Okay then. I need to get down to the NICU. Do you want to walk with me?"

She hadn't really gotten the chance to visit

with Grace so she walked back to the NICU with him. Once there, she met Doctor Peter Kelly, then while the neonatologist conferred with Doctor Prentice, Sarah took the opportunity to bond some more with her baby girl. The open bed gave her so much more access it excited her. They would no longer be separated by a barrier of plastic. And someday soon, she might even get to hold her child in her arms.

Sarah stood looking down at Grace. Bending, she let the baby hold her hand. Grace's tiny hand was the size of Sarah's thumb and seemed to instinctively curl around it. Nurses in the NICU in West Virginia said it was reflex only but Leslie acted as if Grace really knew what she was doing. Eyes tearing, she whispered, "Bye, baby girl. Mommy's going to find a way to keep you here in Philadelphia. I'll be back later and you'll be here waiting for me," she assured her child. It was her standard leave-taking—something of a ritual she hoped would one day be a thing of the past.

Sarah stood straight then and took a deep fortifying breath before forcing herself to step away, once again leaving her child behind.

If only God hadn't turned a deaf ear to her pleas that horrible night when she'd awakened in labor. If only she could be *sure* Grace would live to grow up and that Sarah would find a way to give her a good life.

All afternoon Kip hadn't been able to get Sarah and Grace Bates out of his mind. Had Prentice okayed the surgery? Were they even now operating? Was Sarah waiting alone for word on her child?

He tried not to get involved with the families or the patients he transported, but all his rules had dissolved the moment he'd met Sarah and Grace. He told himself it was just the time of the year getting to him. That it was the approaching holidays making their story seem so compelling and heart-tugging.

Whatever the reason, he finally gave in and admitted he had to know what had happened. The trip into the city wasn't easy even though Philly's nearly four-hour-long rush "hour" shouldn't be a problem on a Saturday. But a great deal of holiday traffic was apparently headed to the large center city shopping district. He arrived at CHOP after dark and went to the NICU first. He talked to one of the nurses he knew, and learned that Grace was there and not in an OR. Of course, the nurse couldn't release any more information than that, so he walked across the street to the hotel to talk to Sarah.

Dressed in lights and Christmas decorations, the street was quieter than usual. The students had deserted the University of Pennsylvania campus, gone home for their winter holiday. And the shopping district was across the river, twenty or so blocks away. Right then the hospitals and hotels were the major draw in this neighborhood.

As Kip approached the front doors of the hotel, Sarah stepped outside. Just seeing her delivered a sharp blow to his stomach. She really was lovely. He was tempted to turn away—to flee—but he noticed she had stopped just outside the door to look at a newspaper she had folded in fours. Her purse hung loosely on her arm and she seemed completely absorbed in the paper, unaware of her surroundings. Unaware of the hidden dangers that could be lurking in the shadows.

Philadelphia was a big busy city with more than its fair share of crime even on the University of Pennsylvania's well-patrolled campus. Didn't she know she had to be on guard in a big city like this?

"Sarah," he called out. She looked up, her gaze vague and unfocused. Honestly, the woman was a danger to herself.

"Oh, hi. I didn't think I'd see you again," she said.

"I kept thinking about Grace and what Prentice's verdict was. Surgery or no surgery?"

A look settled onto her face that combined distraction with profound worry. "He says she's too weak now but he'll operate as soon as it's safer." There was a distinct quaver in her voice that went straight to his heart.

Kip had his answer. He should leave right then but he couldn't with her wandering around after dark on the campus, distracted and anxious. She needed to understand that this wasn't Piedmont Point. His friend had recently bought a small bistro not far from there where they could sit and talk. "Have you had dinner?"

"Dinner?" She tilted her head and frowned. "No. Not lunch either now that I think about it."

"Then let's eat together. Come on. You can sit down, relax and tell me what has you so worried."

She gazed longingly across the street. "I was going to eat at the hospital."

Leslie Washington had confided that it was apparent Sarah was worn out from spending all her time in West Virginia at the hospital with Grace. "No disrespect toward CHOP but over there it's either the cafeteria, which is probably closed now, or the fast-food joint in the lobby. Too much noise and too many kids running around for adults to talk and we need to talk." He took her arm, trying to ignore the urge to put a protective arm around her. He'd just see she got a meal, relaxed for a little while and developed a little sense of self-preservation. Then he'd be outta there.

"Come on. It's just around the corner."

On the way to his friend's bistro, Kip noticed Sarah kept glancing down at the newspaper. His gaze followed hers. The paper was folded to the classified adds. When she dropped it on the table between them as she settled in the quiet booth, he noticed several items were circled. He looked up and saw that she'd let her head drop back against the high back of the banquette and closed her eyes.

Kip picked up the paper. She had rental properties circled. Really cheap rentals that made him suspicious of their locations. "What's with the apartment ads?"

She opened her eyes. They reminded him of rich dark chocolate. "Doctor Prentice confirmed what I'd been thinking about the hospital where Grace was born. She can't go back there."

"So you're staying in Philly?"

She nodded. "Since I can't take her back there and the nearest children's hospital is hours away from Piedmont Point anyway—" She shrugged and took a deep breath as if steeling herself to voice her decision once again. "Yes. I've decided to stay here."

Kip was more worried about her than ever. Which worried him on a whole other score. Why did this woman and her problems tempt him to break all his long-standing rules? "That's a big step. Is there any way I can help?" he found himself asking.

What was he doing? Making sure she had a good meal and understood about moving safely through the city was one thing. Any more would be too much. Too close. He had a score of married female friends whom he either worked with or who were married to his friends, but he steered clear of single women in solitary activities unless it was crystal-clear they were buddies like he and Joy Peterson, his partner, had been. It was a personal rule he never broke. Especially when the woman produced in him a distinctly un-buddylike attraction.

Okay. There. He'd said it. He was attracted to her. He'd been feeling it from the moment he'd seen her standing frozen in place outside the plane in West Virginia. And the pull he'd felt had only increased with everything he learned about her.

This wasn't a good idea.

Not for him.

And especially not for her.

He shouldn't continue to be part of Sarah's life. He'd once inadvertently hurt a woman he'd been dating. He'd met her at his church singles group. She'd fallen in love with him when all he'd ever wanted was simple friendship. He'd never even kissed her but she'd thought he was gallant by holding off on emotions he'd never have let himself feel. And she hadn't only had her feelings hurt. She'd been devastated. Kip had felt so badly that he'd changed churches so she wouldn't feel uncomfortable seeing him all the time.

He'd seen his sisters and cousins hurt over the years by guys who didn't share their feelings. When he'd found himself responsible for breaking someone's heart, it had really disturbed him. Kip's conviction about marriage, leaving a woman burdened financially and grieving and his feelings about passing his genes on to his sons ran too deeply in him to be ignored. Consequently, he never dated. He would never chance hurting someone like that again. And he certainly wouldn't do what his dad and uncle had.

But when he thought of Sarah exiting the hotel in her distracted frame of mind, he shuddered inwardly. His mother would call her a babe in the woods. And she'd be right. If he didn't offer her help, it would be like abandoning a child in the middle of a mine field. So he jumped in. "These are pretty low-end apartments you circled."

She shrugged. "It's what I can afford. Maybe after I get a full-time teaching job and a little savings stored up again, I'll be able to get a bigger place."

Kip put the paper on the table between them again, pulled out a pen and his cell phone. Five minutes later, after several calls, he'd crossed out half of those she'd circled. "Look, I can't afford to be picky," she finally protested.

"These aren't cheap because they're small

apartments. They're cheap because they're in really bad neighborhoods. Neighborhoods where no one lives safely. Where kids have been shot playing in front of their houses. Killed watching television in the living room."

Sarah's eyes widened. "But this is a beautiful city."

"I'm not saying a lot of it isn't wonderful. But this isn't small-town USA. This is a big eastern city." He took the paper and circled the places that by the high-end pricing he assumed were in acceptable areas. "These are probably small apartments in center city or in other high-end sections of the city." He pointed to the first one she'd circled. "This one's probably a whole floor of a huge home but it's in heavy drug territory and there've been several home invasions around there." He ran his finger down the column. "And here there were several drive-by shootings last month…all of which were drug related." He moved to the top of the next column then looked back up at her. "Should I go on?"

Her dark eyes looked troubled. "But those were the only ones I could afford until I get a job. Other people live in those neighborhoods. I'll just have to be careful and make sure I can move before Grace comes home."

It was on the tip of Kip's tongue to promise to help her solve her problems. But he hesitated again. Did he have the right to become involved in her life? Thinking of the places she'd circled, the question he had to ask himself was, did he have a right to let her try navigating the mean streets of Philly alone?

He'd prayed that someone would enter Sarah's life to give her the support she needed but that someone wasn't supposed to have been him. On a mental sigh, he admitted he had no choice. He had to offer help.

His friend and pastor always said the Lord had a weird sense of humor. It seemed once again Jim had been proven right!

And this time the joke was on Kip!

Chapter Three

"I think I have a solution to your problem," Kip said and prayed he wasn't creating a bigger one for himself.

But rather than calming her down, Kip could feel Sarah's anxiety heighten. "I hate to be a bother," she said. "You've done so much for us already by flying Grace here on your holiday weekend and helping pay for my hotel room, too."

Had his reluctance to get involved shown? He felt small and mean. "It isn't a bother," he told her, meaning it. "It'd help my sister out, too. She'd be part of the solution. Miriam lives out in the suburbs and she has this cute apartment over her garage. She's rented it in the past but she had trouble with her last tenant. My brother-in-law travels a lot, and he's leery of renting it again with his wife and kids subjected to a tenant he doesn't know. But *you'd* be the perfect neighbor."

"Wouldn't it cost more than those?" she asked, pointing to the paper on the table between them.

"I don't think so. It's a little small and only one bedroom but it'd give you a start. It's close to public transportation, too, so you could get here pretty quickly and easily."

"But one of the nurses told me that to teach in Philadelphia you have to live in Philadelphia. I have a much better chance of getting a job in a big city."

"There are plenty of schools along the same transportation line that runs near Miriam's place."

Then it came to him. The art teacher at Tabernacle Christian School was leaving on maternity leave soon. The Lord did indeed work in mysterious ways. "I just remembered that our pastor's looking for a long-term substitute teacher to take over our art program for the rest of the year. The regular teacher is going out on maternity leave.

"And there's another plus. My sister with the rental is the first-grade teacher at Tabernacle Christian. She could give you a lift to and from school everyday and save you transportation costs. I'd bet Miriam's place might wind up to be cheaper in the long run. There's no city wage tax and car insurance rates are much lower out in the 'burbs. Should I give her a call and see what she says?"

"I-I don't know." Sarah frowned. "I couldn't accept charity. You'd have to ask her up front what she charges."

He nodded and hit Miriam's speed dial on his cell. His sister answered on the first ring. "Mir, you still holding off on that apartment rental?"

Sarah watched as a wide smile curved Kip Webster's full lips. He honestly was movie star handsome but in a boy-next-door kind of way. There was goodness in Kip's heart that shone like a beacon the same way his Christian principles did. Even though she was angry at God for Grace's problems and a whole list of other things, Sarah knew that following His ordinances was the best way to live. She wished her anger would just go away. It hurt worse than any kind of loneliness she'd ever experienced to be so separated from the Spirit of the Lord. Almost every time she was worried or had a decision to make, she started to pray but then she'd remember...

She remembered the fear and pain of the night she'd awakened alone, frightened and in labor. At twenty-three weeks into her pregnancy Sarah had known Grace was in severe trouble. She'd called out for God's help. She'd begged Him to stop her labor, but He'd turned His back on her, and now Grace's life hung in the balance every minute of every day. That was awfully hard to forgive on top of losing Scott and her parents failing her over and over again.

"Did you hear me?" she heard Kip ask.

Sarah blinked and focused on his concerned expression. She must have looked like a lunatic staring right at him but not following his conversation at all. "I'm sorry. I was thinking about Grace," she explained but left out her crisis of faith and her reasons for it. She was honestly ashamed of her anger and doubts, but she couldn't seem to get past them, either.

"Try to believe that everything will turn out okay," he said. He reached over and covered her hand with his and gave it a quick squeeze before letting go.

Sarah was shocked by the strange tingle

that chased up her arm at his touch. Every thought in her head fled, her stomach seemed to bottom out and her heart leapt in her chest. Her response took her by surprise. Even with Scott she hadn't felt this kind of unmistakable attraction. She fought to get her thoughts back in order. "I do believe it's all going to work out. But until I met Doctor Prentice no one else agreed."

"I have a good feeling about Grace and your move here," he told her. "Everything in life happens for a reason. I know it must be hard for you to see that right now, but give it time."

She nodded but just didn't believe in God's goodness the way she used to.

"Miriam's more than willing to rent to you." He named a low figure she found hard to believe and then continued, "Suppose we go see Grace then run out to take a look at the place."

She felt a moment's panic. She should take time to think about this. She'd gone along with Scott and look what had happened. But then again had she not married him, she wouldn't have Grace and she wouldn't wish her baby away no matter what. "This is all happening awfully fast," she told Kip.

Kip grinned and shrugged his shoulders. "I'd guess that's because the Lord's hand is in it." He picked up a menu and waggled his eyebrows. "So, have you had a real Philly cheese steak yet?"

Two hours later Kip pulled to a stop in a driveway next to a big rambling white clapboard farmhouse. It had a wrap-around porch, colonial mullioned windows and a towering tree on the front lawn. The porch was lined with small white lights and a blow-up snow globe depicting the nativity sat on the lawn below it.

Everywhere Sarah looked she was reminded that Christmas was on the way. She sighed. This certainly wasn't the way she'd pictured Christmas this year. She was supposed to have been able to sit in front of her Christmas tree and tell her healthy newborn the Christmas story for the first time. She'd even decided to leave her tree up longer if Grace came late.

Shaking her head, Sarah got out to look around the quiet, festive looking neighborhood. Then she glanced back up at Kip's sister's farmhouse. "This is almost like a peek back in time. It's wonderful."

"Miriam's is the only really old, really big house on the street. All the others are smaller bungalows or Cape Cods built in the early fifties. The people who used to own this house owned all the land around here. That's why the garage has an apartment. It used to be a carriage house back in the day. Apparently an employee lived up there. I rented it for a few years in my early twenties. Like I said, it isn't much but…"

"Are you bad-mouthing your first bachelor pad?" a disembodied female voice said from the direction of the front porch.

"Mir, what are you doing out here?" Kip asked.

"I have Justine and Bill's kids overnight, remember? I just got them settled. I don't want them to find out their Pied-Piper uncle is here or they'll never get to sleep."

"Oh. I forgot how late it is. They're in bed already."

As Miriam came toward them, Sarah took a few moments to contemplate Kip. She had been able to hear disappointment in his voice because he'd missed seeing his sister's children. She wondered if he loved kids as much as he seemed to, why he wasn't married with a bunch of his own. He was certainly good-looking enough to attract all manner of female attention. He'd certainly grabbed hers and she wasn't looking for complications after losing Scott and being left to care for Grace alone.

Kip gestured toward the small woman who now stood in front of them. "Sarah, this is my oldest sister, Miriam Castor. Mir, this is Sarah Bates."

When Miriam stepped out of the shadows into the patch of driveway lit by a decorative lamppost, Sarah was a bit surprised. She looked nothing like Kip. Her red hair blazed like fire in the bright lamplight and her redhead's complexion glowed. Plus his big sister was tiny. Shorter even than Sarah who was only five foot four inches tall herself. Miriam was also quite a bit older than Kip. Not only did brother and sister not look like siblings, they didn't look as if they were even from the same family.

"Sarah, welcome," Miriam said, reaching out to take Sarah's hands in hers. "It's wonderful to meet you. Let's go take a look and you can tell me what you think of the place."

They followed Kip's sister up a sturdy set of wooden stairs on the outside of the clapboard garage and stepped inside the apartment. Sarah walked behind Miriam across a darkened room she assumed was a living area and into a small galley kitchen. Miriam switched on the overhead light and Sarah smiled, liking the homey room. While not the latest thing in decorating, it was certainly more updated than her apartment in Piedmont Point had been. "This is lovely," she told Miriam.

"After the last tenant left, we were doing our kitchen over so we swapped out the range and refrigerator and the best of our old cabinets. I painted them, Gary installed new laminate counters and voila. I hope yo—" Miriam stopped midword as she turned around. She stared at Sarah.

Her frank assessment left Sarah wondering if she had ketchup on her face or shirt from her adventure into what Kip called a cheese steak. "Is something wrong?"

Miriam grinned then; her green eyes looked to be sparkling with mischief. "Not a thing," she said. "In fact, I'd say everything's finally going just perfectly. I really hope you decide to take it." There seemed to be an odd lilt in her voice besides the glee in her gaze, but it was hard for Sarah to be sure since they'd only just met.

Miriam looked over Sarah's shoulder and said, "Kip, go put the light on in the bedroom? And there's a lamp and a table in the closet in there. Could you set it up in the main room?"

There was a long silence from Kip. Sarah could tell he hadn't moved so she turned toward him, curious. Kip stood staring at his sister, his lips pressed in a thin line, his gaze sharp and annoyed. "Don't, Miriam. I mean it."

"For goodness' sake, *what* is your problem? Light the place up so this nice young lady can see all my hard work. How is she supposed to make a decision on an apartment she can't see?"

He huffed out a breath and pivoted away, all but stalking into what she assumed was the bedroom. She heard him mutter, "You know exactly what my problem is."

Sarah wished she knew what had changed her kind, smiling knight into a grumpy, grumbling ogre. But Sarah was out of her element. She didn't really know either of them and had never had a brother or sister so sibling dynamics were beyond her.

"Am I causing a problem between you two? Please don't feel obligated to rent to me if you don't want to."

"Don't be silly. Kip vouched for your character and I'd love to help out the widow and child of a vet. It's our duty to help the wives and children of our fallen servicemen."

The light flickered on in the bedroom then and Kip returned after a moment to set up the table and lamp. He lit the room, and Sarah fell in love with it. She stood speechless in the kitchen doorway. The white trim shone against creamy caramel-colored stucco walls that picked up on the deeper tones in the hardwood flooring. There was a fieldstone fireplace in the same creamy caramel colors. And the kitchen walls and cabinets were a shade or two lighter, creating a nice continuity between the rooms.

A clatter in the kitchen drew Sarah's attention back to Miriam. "We took out part of this wall and put these shutters here," the older woman explained. "That way if you don't want the kitchen open to the big room you can close it off. But if you like, you can also leave them open when you're entertaining. Gary added this countertop on the pass-through so with a couple high stools on that side, it can be used as a breakfast bar." She walked around the partition and pointed to a door. "That door over there leads to an interior set of stairs. You can use them when it's raining or snow is all over the outside ones. My kids tend to just dump their bikes where they don't belong so I'd avoid them whenever you can till the kids get used to being careful again."

She went on to rattle off a few facts on the kind of heat and cooking the place had, pointing out a microwave and exhaust hood combination over the stove. She explained how to operate the dishwasher. Sarah realized that the way Miriam talked the rental was a done deal.

Sarah didn't say anything. Her head was still in a bit of a whirl over how quickly this move to Pennsylvania had fallen into place. Could it be that God's hand really *was* on her and Grace in spite of all that had gone wrong and in spite of Sarah's anger at Him? She wished she could believe it. But she could no longer make so easy a leap of faith no matter how much she wanted to.

She followed Miriam across the large room. Sarah knew she was sold on the place before she even reached its single bedroom but then Miriam pointed out a deep alcove at the far end of the bedroom. Inside the alcove was a small octagonally shaped window.

"I could put Grace's crib in there," she said and even she heard the dreamy tone in her own voice.

"It'll happen," Kip said immediately.

Sarah blinked. How could he know what she'd been thinking? And there was once again his confidence in Grace's outcome. It never failed to boost her spirits. He talked about Grace's future with such assurance it was as if he had already seen it. His belief bolstered her own hopes for her child.

"What a perfect idea," Kip's sister said and stepped into the alcove Sarah now realized was formed by two deep closets on either side. "In fact, I have an old screen in the attic you could paint up and set up right here at the front of the nook. That way you could come and go from the bathroom and from bed without her seeing you. To her it'll seem as if she has her own little room." She pointed up to a plant hook. "There's even a place to hang a mobile."

"And I can walk to the train from here?"

"It's about a ten-minute walk. And I hope you don't mind but I called Jim Dillon, the pastor of The Tabernacle. He's the one who hires teachers for the school our church sponsors. He wants to meet you as soon as possible. It seems as though the gal going on maternity leave is anxious to stay home with her feet up. She's having a rough time of it, poor thing."

Sarah's nerves had just settled and now the butterflies took flight again. She hadn't been sure about teaching in a Christian school again. She felt like a bit of a fraud considering her own faith issues. But it was only a temporary position and Scott's GI insurance hadn't amounted to all that much. She needed to get back to work and soon.

"If you give me his number, I'll call and try to arrange an interview."

"Oh, that's not necessary. You hadn't planned to see your daughter again tonight, had you?"

Sarah frowned. Where was this going? "No. I think I'll just go back to my room so I can get a fresh start on the day tomorrow."

Miriam leaned against the window frame and crossed her arms. "Then why not stay with me tonight. I'll take you to church with us in the morning. You can talk to Jim after the service."

"But I can't just—" Sarah began.

Miriam shook her head. "Believe me, I can use a little help corralling my kids and my sister's or I'll never get to services on time. Gary wasn't supposed to still be out of town tonight."

"But church? *And* an interview?" Sarah looked down at the T-shirt and jeans she wore beneath her car coat. "I-I can't go like this."

Kip, who'd been as quiet as a clam said, "You won't stick out dressed like that at our church. Did you bring anything with you from West Virginia you'd feel was more appropriate?"

Sarah blushed. "No. I didn't think to pack anything for church. Everything happened so fast and I usually spend all my time at the hospital. I guess I'll need to buy some things until I can get back to Piedmont Point to get my clothes."

"We'll handle that when the time comes," Miriam chimed in. "In the meantime, I have a few things you'd probably be able to wear if Pastor Jim hires you. And as for the jeans, Jim Dillon lives in them and preaches in them. There was probably a time he slept in them. I'll call and warn him that the interview will be informal. He'll thank you. I've never seen a man more resistant to wearing suits and ties." She grinned. "Except my baby brother. He once really did try to sleep in that jacket of our grandfather's."

Kip sighed. "I should have warned you. My big sister has tried to run everyone's life since Mom moved to Florida with her new husband."

Miriam shot Kip an annoyed look but must have seen the truth in what he said because she blushed and said, "I'm sorry, Sarah. You do what you think is best and I'll be glad to help any way I can."

Sarah had to admit Miriam was right. If she stayed, she wouldn't have to find her own way to the school for her interview. Plus Kip wouldn't have to drive her all the way back to the city. That meant she wouldn't need to sit next to him trying to keep from letting him know the unsettling effect he seemed to have on her. It was something she'd never experienced to this magnitude before and she didn't really know how to handle it.

She was still a bit hesitant about the whole church thing, though. She hadn't been to church since she'd gotten so angry at her pastor after Grace's premature birth. But

Miriam's solution was the most practical. "As long as you're sure the pastor won't be insulted by what I'm wearing," Sarah said finally.

Kip chuckled. "Trust me on this. Our church *and* Jim really are informal but Miriam can lend you something if it'll make you feel more comfortable."

"And he won't mind scheduling a last-minute interview?"

"Honey, he's dying to meet you," Miriam assured her.

Kip left after Miriam confirmed the interview, then she gave Sarah a quick tour of her big colonial farmhouse. After that they talked over the lease and utilities costs on the apartment. Sarah found herself excited about the move. She really loved the little place and was sure it would be perfect for her. She'd be able to make a cozy little home for herself and eventually even Grace. All she had to do was find a way to transport her things to Pennsylvania and make a trip or two to some thrift shops to replace things too bulky to bring with her.

As she settled in to sleep on the sofa bed in a small den on the first floor of Miriam's home, Sarah thought again of the coming interview. She hoped she would be as glad to meet Pastor Jim Dillon as both Miriam and Kip were that she'd agreed to their spontaneous plan.

But it was Kip Webster that dominated her thoughts as she waited for sleep. Normally she was so tired by the end of a day that sleepiness descended over her quickly. This night, despite her busy day, thoughts of a handsome man with an infectious grin, kind eyes and a good heart had questions swirling through her mind.

Questions like how long her loyalty to Scott's memory bound her to the lonely life his death had condemned her to? Questions like why it had been Kip who'd volunteered to ferry her and Grace to Pennsylvania for Angel Flight East? And why meeting him had caused so many things to fall into place for her?

Sleep finally claimed Sarah but not until she admitted to herself that only the future would answer her questions.

Chapter Four

Sarah pulled the passenger side door of Miriam Castor's Ford Expedition closed behind her and took a tired breath. When Miriam had told her she could use help getting her and her sister's broods ready for church, she hadn't been kidding. While trying to help out, Sarah had begun to feel more like a cowboy corralling errant calves than a schoolteacher.

Miriam had five children and her sister had five, as well. Hectic was a kind description for making sure ten energetic children and adolescents were ready for church on time.

"Does everyone in your family have a lot of children?" she asked once she and Miriam both got their breath.

Miriam smiled. "Everyone but Kip. He isn't married and says he never will be."

"Isn't that what all men say? Then they meet the right person and change their minds," Sarah said and yawned.

No answer came from Miriam's side of the big SUV's front seat, drawing Sarah's undivided attention. Their gazes collided. Kip's sister looked a bit irritated, leaving Sarah thinking she'd said something wrong. As Miriam turned around to check that all the seat belts were buckled, Sarah saw that a hint of a smile tipped her lips up at the corners so Sarah relaxed.

Once they were on the road, Miriam finally said, "Kip says wanting to stay single is because of the way we grew up."

Sarah remembered Kip and his reaction to Grace. It made no sense. The man clearly loved children. "If it's not too personal a question, what about the way you grew up would make him feel that way?"

"Both our father and uncle died rather young. My mom was barely making it financially when our uncle died. My aunt just wasn't equipped to support six children alone and there was no way they were going to survive. We all moved in together. It was a good solution for our mother and aunt but made for a wild scene sometimes. I'm afraid living in a household with four older sisters and six girl cousins who were both older and younger than him, a mother, an aunt, and a grandmother made Kip sick of putting up with women, kids and chaos."

To Sarah that kind of chaos sounded like heaven but she could imagine Kip had felt constantly outnumbered. "I hardly had a family at all," she told Miriam. "I spent a lot of time in boarding schools and with teachers and friends at the holidays."

"Where were your parents?"

Sarah sought a light tone. "My parents are missionaries. They didn't take me on the more dangerous assignments. As time went on, more and more mission trips were to troubled parts of the world. So I went along less and less." Wanting to get off the subject of her dismal childhood, Sarah said, "I'm surprised to hear Kip is against a marriage and children. He was so natural with Grace and believe me no one other than medical people have ever been anything but shocked or horrified when they first see her."

"Oh, he's great with kids. But he says it's fun to be their adoring uncle, or to coach or to mentor. He just wants the freedom to hand them back when he's had it. I'm hoping he'll change his mind about marriage and a family someday. I hate that he's so alone in the world."

Miriam steered the big SUV onto a narrow road with practiced ease and just as smoothly changed the subject. "So you never told me how you liked teaching at a Christian school in West Virginia instead of a one-room school on the African plains."

At least this was a safer subject than her life with and without her mother and father. "It's different there. Yet, in many ways, it's the same. All children have pressures on them to conform to their secular culture's vision of the world. Here it's music, dress and sex. Over there it's some of that and other cultural pressures, too."

"What about hunger and poverty?"

"Poverty is what they consider normal. Every student felt honored just to be able to come and learn and that's the biggest difference. Don't get me wrong. There were a lot of eager students in West Virginia but there were a tragic few who weren't motivated to do more than take up space. I wasn't prepared for that."

Miriam shook her head sadly. "I see it, too, even in the early grades."

"I almost think it's harder than it is to have them come to school hungry. I gave them my lunch in Doctal. The problem here isn't so easily fixed."

"But it can be fixed. It just takes time and a lot of patience," Miriam put in. "Pastor Jim takes troubled kids on as a personal mission because his older sister died of a drug overdose. He's gotten Kip involved, too. So far they've had great results."

"What if the troubled child is a girl?" she asked. She'd love to help troubled girls but in a Christian school she could only do that if she could get her own faith issues worked out. How in good conscience could she tell a troubled child to pray for guidance or better circumstances when she didn't believe it herself.

"Holly Dillon, Pastor Jim's wife works with them, along with a few of the women in the church."

"Your pastor sounds so different from any minister I've ever met," Sarah said, feeling her nerves grow taut again. One good thing with the hectic morning had been that there hadn't been time to get anxious about interviewing with this paragon Kip and Miriam never stopped praising.

"Pastor Jim isn't exactly one of a kind," Miriam admitted, then she smiled fondly. "but he's one of a very special breed. His life is touched by the Lord's grace, that's for sure. I'm frequently surprised to see him apply a millenniums-old biblical principle to life today and have it fit as if it were written for today. He's opened more than one heart to the truth."

The man sounded bigger than life. And as if he'd be able to see right through her to all her flaws. Sarah felt her nails digging into her palms. What if he saw her anger at God and called her on it? What would she say? How could she explain jealousy and anger at her Lord when she couldn't even understand it herself?

Kip walked into the church's sanctuary and found himself swamped by several members of his football team. They'd played their last game on Thanksgiving morning and had trounced the other team for the division championship. He'd thought their spirits would still be high but it only took a second to realize what he saw was anxiety, not excitement.

Still, they were all talking at once and creating a commotion. He cringed as calls of "Coach. Coach," seemed to reverberate off the rafters of the converted barn that was now the sanctuary of The Tabernacle. The structure had once housed the church offices, Sunday school rooms and the nurseries too. But the church had grown so large that they'd had to add on to the octagonal barn. Like the spokes of a wagon wheel, corridors led to rooms where those extra functions now took place and the sanctuary had been expanded to encompass the whole original building.

"Hey, guys, quiet it down a little," Kip told the teens. Once that was accomplished he continued, "Now what are you all trying to tell me?"

He still didn't catch which one of them was saying what but he put it all together. Aidan Graham, the school's volunteer basketball coach, had been in a car accident the night before.

"He like totaled his car," his second-string quarterback lamented.

"Harry, he nearly totaled himself," Pastor Jim Dillon's son Ian said. At sixteen the kid still carried a hint of an accent. He'd been born and had lived several years in New Zealand where his parents met while Jim was in the navy. They'd divorced when Ian was an infant and before Jim found the Lord. Love for their child and each other had brought them together again. Now, some years later, they had several more children and were the happiest couple Kip had ever seen.

"Is Aidan going to be all right?" Kip asked Ian.

The sixteen-year-old grimaced. "He broke a lot of bones. One leg in several places. He'll be out of work for a while. My dad was at the hospital till late last night. He says Coach Graham will need quite a bit of rehab but he's going to be okay."

"The thing is," Harry put in, "now we've lost our B-ball coach and practice starts next week. If we don't have practice, we'll never be ready to start the season."

Now Kip understood the mobbing. They wanted him to coach in Aidan Graham's place. He probably would but they needed to understand that it was Aidan and not a game that really mattered. "There are more important things than playing ball, guys. Maybe the team just shouldn't have a season."

One of the four, a tall blonde, nodded, shamefaced. "That's what Ian said, but if we don't play all the other teams are going to have holes in their schedule. And they all depend on ticket sales to fund their teams. Plus some of the seniors are hoping for scholarships. If the scouts can't see us play they can't be impressed."

Ian nodded. "Dad said he'd help but he has so much to do already. And coaching is a vast commitment. I don't know where he'd get the time to be the *head* coach. If he only had to be the assistant, though..."

Kip sighed. "Okay. I'll do it." He held up his hand before they could cheer. "But we're going to need to lend a hand at the Graham house. His house will need winterizing and Aidan's mother and father are elderly and can't be raking leaves and shoveling out that driveway once snow starts. That was Aidan's job and we'll have to do it."

The boys all nodded.

"And if his recovery goes into spring, we'll still need to take care of the physical things he can't."

They all nodded and Ian said, "I'll tell my dad he doesn't need to find a head coach and that the team plans to handle the outside work at Coach Graham's house till he's back on his feet."

Kip gave Ian a sharp nod. "You do that," he said and watched the boys head back out of the sanctuary. And then his eyes fell on Sarah Bates laughingly ushering his younger nieces and nephews in the front door and on down the first corridor toward their class-rooms. His sister walked in behind her with the fourth- through eighth-graders who'd need to use the next corridor. When Miriam and the older kids passed from his line of sight, Kip's eyes returned, as if by their own volition, to Sarah distributing the children at the doors of their classrooms.

A longing like none he'd ever felt swept through him. He was always aware of a certain emptiness in his life but for the most part he filled it with his job, friends, Angel Flights and coaching. Often, when he'd get home to his place, he'd feel a void like a heaviness in his heart but it would soon pass when he sank into his favorite chair to read the Word. Never before, in the midst of one of the activities he'd used to fill his life, had he been struck with this hollow pain.

The feeling was as unwelcome and dis-turbing as Miriam's comment when she suddenly tapped him on the shoulder. "Mom would say you're woolgathering. I think you see something you want. Finally. She's such a sweet person."

His sister was scarier than his mother with her ability to read expressions. Kip pressed his lips together and took a moment before speaking. "I'm not having you throw Sarah at me. It's cruel. I may be coaching basketball which means we may be working at the same school if she gets the job. She doesn't need you embarrassing her and I don't need it either. She has more heartache than she can handle already. Not only is her baby's future up in the air but she's a recent widow."

"She's a widow who was so lonely that she only knew the guy she married for three months. For all intents and purposes their marriage only lasted a week. You get over that kind of loss a lot easier than you do a long and happy marriage. Except for her baby, that girl is all alone in the world and has been for what sounds like most of her life. And I don't think she likes it."

"Then I'm sure the Lord has a great guy out there for her but *he* isn't going to be *me*."

He saw Sarah walking up to them and realized from the look on her face that his expression reflected his annoyance. He quickly plastered on a smile and turned a bit more toward her. "Hi, Sarah. All ready for your interview?"

"I hope so," Sarah said but looked unsure. He hoped his mood hadn't influenced hers. "I still feel underdressed," she added and looked down at the peasant skirt and T-shirt she must have borrowed from Miriam.

Just then the three guitarists on stage struck the first chords of an upbeat hymn and the drummer and keyboard player joined in. It was the way the music ministry called the Tabernacle's members to worship. Jim Dillon stepped inside a door on the far side of the sanctuary then. He was dressed as always in jeans and a casual shirt. He waved to Kip, his worn bible in his hand. His smile was as always, kind and welcoming.

Kip heard his sister point Jim out to Sarah. She said she was relieved to see that he didn't float six inches off the ground. Maybe in trying to relax her they'd puffed up Jim's worth a bit too much which he knew Jim wouldn't appreciate.

"Jim would be the first to tell you he's just a regular sinner like the rest of us," Kip commented, hoping to alleviate a little of the worry he'd heard in her voice. He didn't understand her nervousness. Talking to Jim was often comforting, always eye-opening but never stressful. Other than the memory of the father he'd adored, Jim had affected Kip's life as a Christian man the most profoundly.

Kip was often tempted to seek Jim's counsel about the decision he'd made to remain single. But he could see no way Jim could extend his life or change the way he felt about the unfairness of leaving a wife behind, perhaps with a son she would outlive as had been his grandmother's lot in life. To spare loved ones the kind of pain he'd felt, not once but twice, he'd have to continue to deal with his longing for a wife and family of his own. As uncle, coach or mentor—not as husband and father. It would be fairer to everyone that way.

"We should find a seat," he heard Miriam say. He nodded and followed the two women up one of the aisles.

They sang five praise songs. The congregation clapped and tapped their feet to the upbeat tunes then the praise leader said a prayer calling for God's blessing on all of them. Jim called for prayer for Aidan

Graham after making the announcement about his accident. Then he spoke topically rather than his usual expository teaching style because it was a holiday weekend and so many members were away visiting. He was his usual insightful self, speaking about why bad things happened to good people like Aidan.

He discussed various theories, finally admitting there were no earthly answers. He laughingly confided that he planned to ask the Lord for an answer when he met Him in person. Then he added that he'd probably forget because he'd be standing before the throne and be so awed that it wouldn't matter to him anymore.

"Generally no one who's healthy of mind and body wants to die because, bad as life here can be, it's what we know. If any of us had been given the choice to be born we'd likely have wanted to stay safe and warm inside our mother's womb. What I really think happens is that after we've gone through the process of death, we'll understand that it's no big deal. We'll be happier in the throne room than we were here. Happier than anyone could ever be here on earth."

Kip didn't doubt that. But he still thought he'd remember his big question and still need an answer for it. He wanted to know why some people have so few years on earth when others have so many.

Chapter Five

After the service, Sarah followed Miriam to Pastor Dillon's office. "Pastor Jim, this is Sarah Bates," Miriam said when the pastor greeted them in the hall outside his door.

Jim Dillon put out his hand and Sarah placed her hand in his for a friendly shake. He was a good-looking man. Tall and lean with a little graying at the temples that made him look more approachable than distinguished. His smile widened and the look in his eyes put her instantly at ease. "Sarah Bates, welcome to the Tabernacle *and* Pennsylvania. Come on in and we'll chat about the school, our faith statement, and the particulars of the job. Do you have the application filled out that I faxed over to Miriam last night?"

Sarah handed him the completed application and the resume she'd quickly done up last night, too, then she followed him inside his office. She took a chair across from his desk as he closed the door to the noisy hall. Reading as he walked, he opened a second door to tell someone in an adjoining office that he'd located his applicant in the hall. He came back in and moved to sit behind the desk as a lovely woman with long auburn hair and sparkling eyes entered.

"Sarah, this is my wife, Holly. Sweetheart, this is Sarah Bates, the answer to my prayers."

The look of love that passed between the pastor and his wife made Sarah's heart ache with loneliness.

"It's wonderful to meet Kip and Miriam's friend," Holly Dillon said in sort of a British accent.

"I have to be honest, I'm not really their friend. I only just met both Miriam and Kip yesterday," Sarah explained.

Pastor Jim nodded. "Oh, I know. You were his latest Angel Flight. When I saw Kip on Thanksgiving at the game, he told me all about his plans to fly you and your baby here on Saturday. But friendship isn't a matter of time. Don't you think it's a matter of heart? I've known some people for years but a friendship never clicked between us. I've counseled married couples who dated for years before marriage but they can't get along. On the other hand I've felt comfortable marrying couples who only dated weeks before realizing how much they love each other. They've gone on to have marriages where rarely a cross word passes between them. I think relationships are a matter of heart and whether or not God has ordained them. The problems happen when we try to force a bond."

Sarah nodded. Maybe he was right.

Pastor Dillon looked over her resume as she sat in silence waiting for questions. "Your latest post was at Piedmont Christian School in Piedmont Point, West Virginia but you were only there four and a half months," he said at last, sounding a little concerned. "You seem to lead a very transient life."

"*Too* transient," she admitted before she could stop herself.

Jim Dillon's eyebrows rose. "Are you saying you aren't as nomadic at heart as your school records suggest?"

She forced a smile. "The moves were my

parents' idea. They're missionaries. I thought I wanted to follow in their footsteps, but after working in Doctal for a few years, I realized it wasn't for me."

Sarah didn't add that she'd had spent less than six months in Doctal with her parents. They'd moved there from Darfur to establish a mission and school and had been there for several years when she arrived fresh from college. Then suddenly their sponsoring church asked them if they were interested in opening a new mission field in another part of Africa. They'd jumped at the chance and left her behind once again. She'd stayed in Doctal but, after two and a half years, she'd had enough of the heartbreaking poverty, disease and the growing violence in the country.

"I'd kept in touch with my college advisor," she went on with the part of the story she felt she needed to share. "She recommended me to Piedmont Point Christian where a friend from college already worked. I went there looking for a quiet place to call home. I thought I'd found it and had planned to spend the rest of my life there. Then my husband was killed and Grace was born severely premature."

"That must have been very difficult, especially living among people you couldn't have known very well," Holly said.

Sarah nodded, surprised to have her feelings confirmed by a stranger. It was a confirmation of her right to feelings she hadn't been sure were valid. "I didn't come to Philadelphia with the idea of moving here," she went on to explain, "though I'd begun to suspect I'd have to move for Grace's sake. Her surgeon more or less confirmed what I'd been thinking during a discussion yesterday. I'm confident she'll be better off near the kind of quality doctors they have at Children's Hospital."

Jim and Holly glanced at each other and smiled those special smiles again. "The doctors at CHOP probably saved our oldest son's life and they certainly changed it. He has severe asthma but they helped get it under control."

She nodded. "Then you understand my decision to stay here. Last evening as I was thinking over my next move toward relocating us, I ran into Kip. He noticed the apartments I'd circled in the paper I had with me." She shrugged, still toying with the idea that the Lord had finally taken pity on her and was orchestrating her move. "One thing led to another," she said, unwilling to voice the persistent thought. "Kip told me about your need for a substitute art teacher and about Miriam's apartment. And here I am."

He sat up a little straighter and smiled. "Sometimes the Lord's methods can be pretty forthright." He picked up a piece of paper and handed it to her across the desk. "Here's the Tabernacle's faith statement," he said as she took it. "We don't require our teachers to join our congregation. But we *do* ask that their interactions with students reflect this attitude."

She reviewed it quickly, having already read it in the church bulletin. It stated that they were not a denominational church but a fellowship who believed in the Lordship of Jesus Christ. It said they strove to know Him through the scriptures and the power of the Holy Spirit. She could easily agree to that.

It went on to say they sought to have their worship be flexible to His leading, and placed significant value on the music ministry as a tool of the Lord. She'd enjoyed the music and it had given her a sense of peace, a real accomplishment, considering how nervous she'd been when she'd arrived.

They also emphasized teaching the Word in their services so God could instruct them through the scriptures. She had no problem with any of that.

It was the final part of the statement that troubled her. They believed His Agape love was the basis of Christianity and that its manifestation was evident in the lives of those who believed.

It was exactly what had Sarah questioning God, herself and her faith. Even this man, one of the best representatives of Christ she had ever heard preach, had just admitted at the end of his sermon that he didn't know why God allowed bad things to happen to His people. As far as Sarah was concerned, her whole life had been a roller-coaster ride of one disappointment after another. Was that supposed to be the sign of a loving God working in her life?

Instead of challenging his beliefs, however, Sarah kept silent and nodded as she set the paper on his desk. Her doubts were hers and she *did* need this job, however temporary it was. This would be a good measure of her ability to function in a Christian school again. After talking to Miriam, she realized she might fit in better in a Christian school. If she taught in a public school, she was bound to see more of the sort of behavior that had troubled her about a few of her students back in Piedmont Point.

She and Pastor Jim talked about her teaching experiences and the way she liked to conduct her art room. He explained that she could apply for an emergency teaching certificate in Pennsylvania which would allow her to teach for a year while fulfilling any requirements she was missing in order to get a teaching certificate in the state. He asked if he could contact her school in West Virginia and the missionary board who had sponsored her in Doctal.

Sarah asked him to give her a day to contact Piedmont Point Christian's principal to tell him she wouldn't be coming back.

"Something's changed since Miriam spoke with me last night," Pastor Jim told her then. "Joanne Roberts, the teacher I needed a sub for, stopped by my office after the first service this morning. She and her husband have decided she won't be returning after her baby's born."

"So you only need a sub till you find a permanent replacement, is that it?" She'd really hoped to have till the spring to start an all-out job search.

Holly Dillon sighed and put a hand on her husband's shoulder. "What Jim is trying to say is that if your references check out and if at the end of the year we all agree that Tabernacle Christian School is the place for you, you'll be hired as a full-time teacher."

Sarah blinked. "Oh. I hadn't expected…" Her throat caught as tears welled up. Overcome with the sudden easing of so many burdens, she could only stare at him as more tears gathered and fell.

The pastor looked at his wife in a near panic but Sarah couldn't stem the flow of her tears. Holly sighed. "Go," she ordered him and rushed to Sarah's side as the kind pastor beat a hasty retreat.

"I'm so sorry," Sarah choked out. "I've chased your poor husband out of his own office. He's probably not even going to hire me as a sub now."

"Oh, don't be foolish. That's just Jim being Jim. You'd think after all these years in the ministry he'd be used to a few tears but he can't handle crying women. Or children. Makes for chaos at home when someone gets hurt because he falls apart." She handed Sarah a tissue and patted her back. "Don't worry about it. I'm sure the job is yours. You have every right to a few tears with all Miriam tells me you've been through."

Sarah wiped her eyes and blew her nose. "It's just all been so overwhelming and now, in one day, it feels as if a pressure valve has been opened. I'm still worried about Grace but everything else has just fallen into place. And all because Kip Webster volunteered to fly us here. I don't know how I'll ever thank him."

"Knowing Kip, he doesn't expect your thanks. Helping you would be enough thanks for him. He wouldn't see what he's done as deserving of a lot of notice. He'd see it as being used of the Lord. He's a wonder. So are his sisters. We're all blessed to have them as members."

"I certainly feel blessed by at least two members of the family."

Holly laughed. "Listen to us. What's really happening is we've been blessed by the grace of God. Without Him, Kip wouldn't be the kind man he is; Miriam wouldn't have been so willing to trust you as a renter; and Jim wouldn't have even considered hiring you on their recommendation alone."

Sarah nodded, but a knot of unease formed in her stomach so she said little else. She just wanted to get out of there with what was left of her dignity in place. She wasn't a foolish watering pot. She stood on her own in the world and had survived disappointment and near abandonment at the hands of her parents on and off since she was seven years old. She'd survived heartbreak when Scott was killed. Fear and pain when Grace was born so small and helpless.

Holly said Jim Dillon had decided to hire her but she would never again count on life to work out for her. What was that old saying—*The Lord giveth and the Lord taketh away.* If it was true, He could easily wave His hand and somehow she'd find herself trying to survive in bad neighborhoods with, or worse, without Grace.

Sarah wished with all her heart she could go back to the hopeful, faith-filled person she'd been before Scott's death and Grace's birth. But she felt as if a wall had been erected between her and her Savior. It was perhaps the most desolate feeling she'd ever experienced and she didn't know how to knock that wall down.

These days that hollow emptiness was always there inside her ready to claim her if she let it. If she took this position, she knew it would be harder to drift from day to day, putting one foot in front of the other, and keeping so busy she had no time think. Day in and day out she would be surrounded by evidence of His presence.

But she had no choice. This leg up was too beneficial to turn down. She had to accept the help of these strangers who had happened into her life. She was just too tired to go it alone any longer. And she had to go on. Grace was counting on her to provide a stable life.

For Grace's sake she would walk a road she felt unworthy to set her foot upon.

Chapter Six

Kip pulled his car into a spot next to the playground at the school end of the church property and parked. He had his first basketball practice of the season scheduled for after school. As he got out of his car, the final bell rang and he looked across the lot. Doors in the high school wing opened moments later and the kids came pouring out. Sarah Bates, her chestnut hair blowing in the stiff breeze, pushed open a double set of doors and led a group of small children to the line of school buses waiting to take them home.

It was the first time he'd seen her since she left to talk to Jim after Sunday services the week before. He'd been out of town on a long charter last Sunday so he hadn't seen her at church either. Early last week his friend and pastor had let slip that, when he'd told her the job was hers, she'd begun to cry from sheer relief. Jim had also mentioned that the job might be a permanent one as long as all her references checked out.

Sarah looked at home there among children on that first full day she'd been teaching. He wondered how she'd done. And how little Grace was faring at CHOP.

Kip glanced at his watch. He had a good fifteen minutes before the team was supposed to meet in the gym. He sauntered toward her and arrived as the last child in her charge boarded the bus.

Sarah turned, and a wide smile brightened her face, making her look younger and less burdened. He felt good about that. She deserved any happiness she found after all she'd been through.

"So how was the first day?" he called out to her.

"Wonderful," she said when he reached her side. "I came in for the morning yesterday so I could visit all the classes and meet all of the students. And I observed Joanne in some classes. In the afternoon after I left, she had the classes make welcome cards for me. I'm going to hang them up. I have several from your nieces and nephews. Do you want to see them?"

"Sure," he said and fell into step next to her. "I can even help you for a few minutes. It feels good to be back teaching, then?" he asked her as he pulled open the door to the school and held it for her.

"It feels wonderful to be back teaching. I'd forgotten how much I like it. And since I'll be working K through twelve I'm going to be wonderfully busy."

"Then you don't resent having to work instead of being with Grace?"

She tilted her head in thought and stopped just outside her classroom. "Resent it? No. Scott thought I should stay home when we had children, but I hadn't been sure about that. I really love working with talented kids in the upper grades and trying to uncover talent in the younger ones. Getting them to express their emotions on paper with whatever medium they choose is one of the greatest rewards. Now, I don't have to make a choice between home and school. This is just the way it is."

"That's good then. I thought because you always spent so much time with Grace that you'd be missing her a lot."

"I do miss her but we'll have plenty of time together in the afternoons and the evenings. It's more of a relief than you can imagine having her at Children's Hospital. I can finally trust the people taking care of her. I'm even sleeping better," she admitted.

"Then you think you'll stay in the area?"

"Definitely. Now I just have to figure out how to move some of my things here."

"How much do you have?"

"A small dining room set my parents ordered for us as a wedding gift, some keepsakes, my clothes, and a few things I'd bought for Grace that she won't wear for months and months. There are a bunch of household items that I'd rather not have to replace too. One of the teachers I worked with asked if I wanted to sublet my apartment to her and sell her whatever furniture I couldn't afford to ship. We already got permission for the sublet. Except for a bed I've already bought, I'll do without what I sell to her and replace it a little at a time or from a thrift shop," she explained as she led the way into the school's large art room. It was set up in three sections.

Kip looked around and chuckled at the room. It reminded him of his youngest niece's favorite fairy tale. "This looks like the three bears designed it. Small, medium and large."

Sarah laughed, a musical sound he could probably listen to all day and not grow tired of. "K through twelve," she said, sweeping her hand across the wide room. "It's like a one-room schoolhouse and I'm used to that. I like the interaction between the ages. The little ones really bring out the best in the older ones."

He nodded, seeing her point. "So is the apartment working out okay, even though it's so far from the hospital?"

She nodded. "I'm trying to treat this time the way I would if Grace was in day care. Now that my workday is over here, I'll go into the city to see her instead of picking her up at day care to go home. I come home about seven-thirty or eight. That's about the time she'd probably go to bed anyway. So really, if she were a full-term baby, all I'd be missing is getting her up and ready for the day and a middle-of-the-night feeding." She shrugged. "Those would soon be a thing of the past anyway."

He watched her sort through a pile of pages and marveled at her ability to adapt and adjust to each curve life sent her way. "You're going to be a great mother. You remind me of my mom." She'd been the same way after his father died, unlike Aunt Emily who couldn't have survived without his mother's help and now not without her grown daughters. He smiled, thinking of his capable mother. "Grace is a lucky little girl."

Sarah smiled sweetly and looked up. "Thanks, Kip."

"I wondered if you'd like me to fly you to West Virginia to pick up your things. I'm free this weekend and I'm nearly sure the cargo plane is, too." Before she could protest he held up his hand. "We usually fly patients round trip so, in a way, I owe you a flight."

"Good heavens, Kip, you don't owe me a thing. Your thoughtfulness and generosity have helped change my life and Grace's. I already don't know how we'll ever thank you."

He didn't want her thanks. He just wanted to know she was on the road to a good life with as little hardship as possible. Then he'd be able to go on with his own life, content that she and little Grace were going to be okay on their own. He chalked his fascination with Sarah up to worry for a nice woman who'd had one too many bad breaks. That was what it had to be.

"Thanks aren't necessary," he told her, not for the first time. "Come on, Sarah, you know you don't want to be gone a long time. This way you won't be out of town more than the better part of the day. And think of the expense of shipping all that. Unless you plan to drive a rental truck, there's no cheap solution."

Sarah smirked. "As a matter of a fact, that *was* my plan. I learned to drive a truck while I was teaching in Doctal. If I could get around in that old truck, I can drive anything."

Kip's estimation of her went up another notch but the idea of her on the road from West Virginia to Pennsylvania all alone just didn't sit well. "What if something went wrong with the truck?"

She shrugged, "I'd call a tow truck if I couldn't fix it."

"Doctal again?"

"It was a *cranky* old truck."

"But anything could happen. Everyone isn't trustworthy and you'd be all alone on the interstates."

She seemed to consider that but there was still merriment in her dark eyes. "I learned to fence in boarding school. I was quite good. Suppose I keep my épée in the cab with me."

He couldn't help chuckling. She was different from any woman he'd ever met. "Not a bad plan," he conceded with a grin, "but all teasing aside, you have to admit there's no way you can get there and back without being gone a whole weekend if not longer."

She looked uncertain but then she nodded. "You're right. I really don't want to leave Grace for that long right now and I can't keep wearing your sister's clothes. One of the older girls even remarked that Mrs. Castor has a skirt just like the one I'm wearing. I'd have to make sure my friend and the building's rental agent would be able to meet me at the apartment so I can turn over the key and she can sign the lease. She's even agreed to drive Scott's car out during the Christmas holidays. She's a history teacher and she's always wanted to see Philadelphia. It would make the move here so much easier. I know you don't want my thanks but I am grateful."

He let out a purposely dramatic sigh. "Fine, be grateful. Just agree. I'll pick you up at seven Saturday unless your friend can't arrange the time."

Sarah nodded. "So, are you ready to help with the artwork of all these budding geniuses?" she asked and handed him a fistfull of pushpins.

It was all so uncomplicated until their hands touched. Kip sucked a shocked breath when what felt like a bolt of electricity shot through him.

This isn't good, he thought.

And worse was the surprised gasp from Sarah that told him she'd felt the spark of attraction, too.

Really not good, he added.

Sarah looked away, her hands trembling as she reached for the pile of pictures on her desk. She glanced back up at him, a blush coloring her cheeks. "I…um…I thought I'd hang them sort of mixed up, paying no attention to the age of the artist."

"Okay, let's get this done so you can go see Grace and I can get to the gym for B-ball practice," he grumbled, trying to get hold of feelings he wasn't used to dealing with.

Sarah eyes widened. "Oh, I'm so sorry. I didn't even think about why you were here in the middle of the day. You must be one of the busiest people I know and here I am wasting your time."

He glanced at his watch. "Yeah, I guess I'd really better go. You never know what teenagers will get into if you aren't watching them."

Sarah busied herself with the pictures but sounded confused and unsure of herself. "I'm sure that's true. You're welcome to stop by some other afternoon and see your nieces' and nephews' artwork. One of them is very talented."

"Right," he said backing out of the room. The second he cleared the door he turned toward the gym and rushed away. It wasn't until he was nearly to the gym doors that he realized he was still holding the pushpins that had started all the trouble.

Kip felt like a fool for the way he'd actually run away. Sarah probably thought he'd slipped a cog! He may have even hurt her feelings.

But he'd had to get out of there. Nothing like that had ever happened to him before. He'd realized from the first that Sarah was special and he was attracted to her. But he hadn't been prepared for the depth of that attraction until that innocent touch turned into something so much more.

He enjoyed the company of women but

rarely felt attraction to any them. All the years of lukewarm feelings had lulled him into thinking he was safe from the temptation of desire. He knew he'd better give Sarah Bates a wide berth.

Except he'd just promised to spend hours in a plane with her and help her gather her things from her apartment.

No, not good at all.

Chapter Seven

Early Saturday morning Sarah heard a quiet knock on her door. She knew it had to be Kip. "Coming," she shouted and finished tying the laces of her running shoes. "Calm down," she ordered her pounding pulse. She wished she'd never agreed to this. How was she going to survive hours sitting next to him in a cockpit?

Sarah had no doubt that she'd made a fool of herself with him the other day. And ever since she'd been trying to tell herself that the attraction she'd felt was an aberration. No one felt an electric charge when someone touched them unless it was the result of plain old static electricity.

Unfortunately for that theory, it also had happened the first day she'd met him. It was also unfortunate that there was no carpeting in the art room—nothing, in fact, that would produce the kind of friction to give anyone even a mild charge, much less what she'd felt.

Most unfortunate of all, she'd agreed to this trip before she'd acted like an idiot. If only he hadn't sounded annoyed when he'd reminded her that he didn't have all day to help her. His irritation was the worst part of the whole embarrassing episode because it told her he'd noticed her reaction to him.

And if his annoyance hadn't made it clear enough then what he'd done Thursday made it crystal-clear. All she was to him was a charity case. He hadn't called to confirm as he'd said he would. Instead he'd had an Agape Air secretary call her to verify today's flight as an Angel Flight and to give her the time. Which meant this flight wasn't even one friend doing a favor for another. It was a handout.

Sarah plastered a smile on her face and pulled her apartment door open. "I'm all set," she told Kip and turned back to grab her purse.

"Come on then. The meter's running," he quipped with a kind smile and a gesture toward his big black pickup.

Kip's teasing put her at ease—a little. Maybe he'd forgotten what happened. Or maybe it had meant so little to him it just wasn't worth remembering.

Knock it off! This flight is about Grace, not you.

He was flying Sarah back to West Virginia so she wouldn't be away from her precious daughter for an entire weekend or even longer in order to pack and move her things. She wouldn't let pride or injured feelings get in the way of anything concerning her daughter's welfare.

Kip was a nice man, even if all he felt for her was pity. Besides, he could have been very busy this week and his offer of help could have been about friendship. His easy smile certainly said so. She prayed that was the case even as it stung.

Think of him as the brother you never had, she ordered herself as she pulled the apartment door shut behind her and locked it.

Sarah followed Kip to his extended cab pickup and stopped dead when her hand fell on the passenger side door handle. Sitting in the seat was a stunning blond woman. "I hope you don't mind riding in back," Kip said over the hood. "Joy's way too tall to fit back there. They call this a four-passenger cab but only if two of them are munchkins." He grinned. "Your height qualifies you for back-seat duty today, I'm afraid."

The blonde opened her door then pushed open the door to the back seat that opened in the opposite direction. "Sorry. I've tried to sit back there but, embarrassing as it was, I got motion sick all crunched up like that."

Sarah stood stunned and not really thinking too clearly. Then her brain kicked into gear.

Message received. He brought along his girlfriend and I'm just another passenger.

She forced a smile, desperate to hide a hurt she had no reason to feel. "Don't be silly, I'll be fine back here," she said and climbed in. "The headmistress at the first boarding school I went to had a favorite saying when any of us complained about something. 'Beggars can't be choosers,' she'd say. I'm grateful for any help I can get if it helps me get settled quicker so I can take better care of Grace. Kip's been more than generous with his time. I'll be forever grateful."

And message sent, and received, I hope. I know my place now.

"I told you, I don't want your gratitude," Kip grumbled and put the truck into gear. "Joy agreed to co-pilot. Joy Peterson, meet our passenger, Sarah Bates. Because of the cargo coming back with us, we're flying a bigger plane today, Sarah. We can take more of your stuff that way and I thought you two should finally meet."

So she is your girlfriend and this is your way of warning me off? She felt herself blush. "You're a pilot, too? Do you work with Kip?" Sarah asked the tall blonde since she could hardly voice her real question.

"Joy is my partner," Kip put in. "Or more to the point, I'm hers since she let me buy into Agape Air."

How much more embarrassing could this get? Kip's blonde was also the other person who'd helped pay Sarah's hotel fees. Thank heaven she'd sent the woman a thank-you note, she thought just as Joy turned a bit in her seat and said, "I got your note and the wonderful picture of Grace."

"I wanted you to know that I appreciate all you did. You and Kip."

Kip looked up and into the mirror at her and she prayed her blush had subsided. "I met Joy through the Angel Flight East organization. She and her uncle were trying to build up their airline at the time and I was freelancing. I hired on with her and her uncle. After he retired, she was looking for a partner so I bought into the company."

"It's nice you two have the business to share."

"It's been a godsend to have a partner with the same values as I have to share the responsibility with," Joy said with a bright smile before turning front.

"I'm sure it is," Sarah replied, troubled by her jealousy.

She hadn't realized how much she'd been hoping Kip might turn out to be someone she could build a future with. It wasn't that she felt she needed a man to lean on. It was simply that she needed someone to care for and to care for her other than Grace. She'd been alone for so many years. She also felt unfulfilled and lonely—as if God had intended her to be a *wife* and mother. Not just a single parent.

But that begged the question of why the Lord had let Scott die. Tired of circular thinking, Sarah put her head back and closed her eyes. Hopefully, they'd think she'd fallen asleep because of the early hour.

She found the flight less awkward than she'd thought she would because she sat in one of the passenger seats behind the cockpit separated by a bulkhead. Kip showed her the cargo space before they took off so she'd know how much of her furniture she'd be able to bring. It was clear she'd be able to bring more of her things than she'd dared to hope for. She might not have to sell much at all to her friend Mary Jane, and that would eliminate her need to replace those items in Pennsylvania.

Joy and Kip had managed to borrow a truck through their airport contacts so they all squeezed into the front seat and went right to her apartment.

In the few days between the end of their honeymoon and his departure with his Guard unit, she and Scott hadn't wasted any of their precious time together on moving him in. They'd just stuffed the extra bedroom with all his boxes with the idea that she'd unpack after he left. She'd worked slowly incorporating his things with hers those first few weeks. Then after his death, it had been too painful to go through the rest of his things so she'd moved the rest of the boxes down to the basement. She'd left them packed alongside the empty boxes she'd already unpacked.

Sarah suggested Kip and Joy handle her linens and the kitchen cabinets. She knew she wanted all of that so they wouldn't need her further input. And she hoped that way she wouldn't be intruding on what private time they could find after giving up their day off to help her.

Her friend was waiting for their arrival so after they handled the lease with the superintendent, Mary Jane packed up Scott's clothes and hauled them to her car to drop off at the Salvation Army store. Then she set about packing Sarah's clothes and the few she'd bought for Grace.

Which left Sarah free to retire to the basement storage bin while everyone else worked on the apartment. She unlocked the padlock on the door and took a deep breath before she plunged ahead. It had to be done, she told herself, and there was no sense putting it off.

She opened the first box and found picture albums of Scott's ancestors and some from his childhood. Without looking at them further she scrawled "Keep for Grace" on the top of the box and set it on the floor outside the enclosure.

The next box yielded a surprise cache of

trophies. Soccer. Baseball. Track. Sarah stared at them. She hadn't even known Scott played sports, though most boys did, she supposed. The irony didn't escape her that she knew Kip had played football, basketball and baseball as a boy.

After staring at the big box she sat on the dusty floor and looked at each one, lining them up from smallest to tallest, she decided to keep the first and the most impressive for each sport. The rest, she supposed, were trash. She couldn't donate them. Who'd want trophies with a stranger's name on them, after all? Feeling disloyal yet trying to be practical, Sarah walked them out to the trash container and returned with the empty box.

After labeling it so she could add other mementoes to the few trophies she'd kept for Grace, Sarah moved on. But as she went through more treasures of Scott's childhood, she realized they had no meaning without his input. Half of a rubber ball. A pile of blank postcards. A rock. The list went on.

Sarah stood staring at the things in her hands. How could she just throw out his life? How could she have married him and never bothered to learn what that life had been like? He'd lost his parents in his last two years of high school—one right after the other. Then his much older bachelor brother had moved back to the family home to raise him. He'd loved and honored him only to lose him.

His trophies had stopped with the deaths of his parents. Did that mean he'd no longer played? And why? Had his brother not cared to attend the games? That was why she'd quit the fencing team even though she'd been one of the best they had. It was just no fun if no one was there cheering for you on except the parents of other players who were really cheering for a team win.

When she came to his junior high and high school yearbooks, she slid down the wall again and began searching in earnest for a hint of her husband's formative years.

He looked young, of course, but something was different about him in these early pictures. She touched the photos of him captured by an amateur photographer during a soccer game and on later pages running down a basketball court, his long blond hair streaming behind him or whipping across his face. Then as the high school years progressed and the sports shots continued, his hair got shorter and his smile changed, too. But at least she knew he'd continued to play.

Then she looked again and knew what had changed about him. This was the smile she'd known. She'd always believed it to be carefree. Looking back at the older photos, however, she knew she'd found the difference. The grin he'd worn in those later years hadn't been quite as genuinely carefree.

Lonely.

Scott had been lonely, too.

That was why they'd gravitated toward each other! The other teachers had seen it quickly. "Alike as two peas in a pod," the oldest faculty member had said. Tears Sarah hadn't even realized she'd begun to cry fell onto her hands. Had he loved her or had he been as desperate for someone to count on as she had been? More important, since it was he who had had such little time, had *she* loved him as much as he'd deserved?

Sarah desperately hoped so. She really did. But the fact was, she hadn't been as sure as he'd been about their swift marriage. She remembered the conversation with Jim Dillon about relationships. Which kind of couple would they have been? She shook her head. It didn't matter now. But she had little doubt that though their marriage might have been bumpy it would have lasted because they'd both been equally committed to making it work.

But would they have been happy? Would they have been cheating each other?

Shaking her head, Sarah admitted that while she'd never know for sure, she was afraid they would have been. As it had turned out, though, she would always be grateful to Scott for insisting they marry before his deployment. Their marriage had given her a precious gift—Grace. And hopefully she'd given him a hope-filled and happy last week before he went off to war. It was the least she could do to try to make him seem real to their child when the time came.

So she started again to discover who the father of her baby had really been. The next two boxes she came to were full of old school papers and term papers. She read one entitled: *A woman's role as wife and mother as opposed to corporate executive.* Scott's views *had* been a cloud on their horizon, that was for sure. She hadn't wanted to give up teaching. And now, Grace was surely not going to have her mother twenty-four-seven.

Still, it was a window into the mind of the man Grace would want to know about. She dropped it and one other term paper—a silly one comparing soccer to world politics into the keep box and put the rest aside in the boxes headed for the trash.

Taking a deep breath, she started back in on Scott's boyhood treasures. She picked up the postcards again. Maybe they would correspond to family vacations pictured in the photo albums she'd already packed away. Those she added to the trophies and term papers. But what about the rock, the half of the rubber ball or a piece of tooled leather she'd found under the postcards? She stared at them, clutching them in her hands. How could she glean enough about the life of her child's father from the few remnants he'd left behind? Then it struck her that these might not even be his keepsakes but his brother's. With no family to ask, she had no way of knowing.

"Sarah, are you all right?" Joy Peterson asked.

Nodding, Sarah looked up and wiped her cheeks of tears of frustration she hadn't even realized she'd shed. "I'm just realizing I don't know as much about my husband as I thought. How do I tell Grace that? Scott and I talked all the time but about faith and our work. About world affairs and politics. Books and movies…"

"You talked about the things you cared about as adults?"

Sarah nodded.

"Then you knew him. I knew all about my husband's childhood. His brother and mine were best friends but we fought all the time as kids. Then when I was in the last year of high school we stopped fighting and fell in love but we were still too young. Who we were and what we wanted from life at the time forced us apart. We barely spoke for years until we were forced back together by an Angel Flight and a plane crash on the return trip. That's when we really got to know each other enough to accept each other for who we'd become."

What Joy said about having known the man Scott had become was true enough but it was the here and now that had really grabbed Sarah's attention. "You're married? You're not dating Kip? I'm not cutting in to your alone time?"

Joy Peterson's pretty blue eyes widened and she sputtered out a laugh. "You thought Kip and I…? Oh, no. We're just friends and business partners." Then she frowned. "Did he lead you to believe we were more?"

Sarah thought back. Had he? "I don't think

so. I never really talked to him about the exact arrangements for today. He wasn't even the one who called me to confirm the time we'd leave. It was someone from his office but she said this was an Angel Flight. When he volunteered for today, he didn't mention that he was bringing someone with him. But then there you were. And you both seemed so close. I just thought…" She shook her head and shrugged. "Well, never mind what I thought. I was obviously wrong."

"Kip let someone else call you about today? And she said it was an Angel Flight?"

Sarah felt the blood drain from her head. "Was she wrong? Do I owe you for the plane. I don't know how I'll ever pay—"

"Hey, calm down. Of course you don't owe us. Angel Flight *is* helping with gas costs. But Kip offered the plane and our time to help *you,* not some anonymous patient's mother. In fact, I came down to see if you need help with your storage closet."

Relieved, Sarah took a deep breath and pushed a few hairs off her face that had come loose of her ponytail. "No. I'm nearly done. I have another couple of boxes to go through. The rest are wedding presents and Christmas decorations from Scott's family. I already know I want to bring them if it's at all possible. I'd rather leave furniture than those. I want Grace to have the kind of family Christmas I never did."

"There'll be plenty of room," Joy assured her then sort of clapped her hands. "Okay, then. I left Kip packing pots and pans. Any more empty boxes down here we can use?"

Sarah pointed to a pile of boxes. "Those need to be emptied in the paper recycling container, then we can use them. It's what looks like all of Scott's notebooks from school." She smiled. "Like from eighth grade on. I'm finding my husband was a bit of a pack rat." She picked up the partial rubber ball and a huge dart with a metal tip. "Got any ideas?"

Joy's eyes widened and she grabbed the rubber ball. "Half ball! He must have been raised in Philly."

"I think he was born there but moved to the suburbs when he was in junior high. His junior high yearbooks are from different school systems. What on earth is half ball?"

"A game passed down from father to son." Joy looked around the basement. "Or in my case, father to son and daughter. Daddy didn't figure out I was a girl till the night of my prom. Eureka!" she said over her shoulder as she rushed across the basement to a mop standing in the corner. She unscrewed it from the mop head and turned toward Sarah. With the thin mop handle resting on her shoulder like a batter in a baseball game, she said, "Pitch it to me."

Sarah stared then blinked. "Like with baseball? I warn you I'm not much of a pitcher." But she tossed it as ordered and Joy swung, connecting with the tumbling half ball. Sarah caught it easily as it sailed at her.

"It didn't go very far," she said still perplexed. "Why not use the whole ball?"

Joy walked toward her with the loose-hipped grace of an athlete. "*Because* it didn't go far. It wouldn't break a neighbor's window, and it's harder to roof it, too. It's city-street baseball. Here," she said and handed Sarah the mop handle and pushed her toward the other wall. "You try to hit it."

Sarah walked to where Joy had stood. "I told you I was never into baseball." But gamely she swung anyway. The pole and rubber connected with a now familiar *twap* but it veered left. The half ball tumbled through the air and smacked right into Kip's forehead as he stepped into the basement.

She stared in horror as he blinked and

rubbed his forehead. Then he looked at his feet and grinned. "Half ball?" He stooped to pick it up. "I haven't seen one of these in years."

"Sarah was just learning a little about her husband," Joy explained. "We'll see you upstairs. Kip can help me dump all of the paper into the recycling container." After picking up two of the boxes and resting them on her hip, Joy stopped. "You better now?"

Sarah nodded and glanced down at the half ball. "Thanks. I think I'll keep this after all."

"Sure you will. You're a natural. You can teach Grace one day with her daddy's ball. No reason a girl can't play with her daddy's toys. But I'd lose the lawn darts. They've been taken off the market for kids. Real dangerous."

She looked at the unsafe-looking things again and pitched them into the trash can Kip had brought down with him. Then she picked up the half ball and tossed it into the keep box. Scott must have liked playing the game his father had taught him or he'd never have saved the ball. It was something she could share with Grace about her father.

Now, more than ever, she realized she hadn't known her husband well enough to marry him. But at least by doing what Scott had begged her to do she'd given him Grace to continue his family line. She only wished she didn't have to raise his child alone without the family they'd both longed for.

Chapter Eight

"I want to talk to you," Joy told Kip as she followed him up the stairs and out to the recycling bin.

Kip dumped in the contents of one box and tossed it aside. "What about?" he asked and turned toward his partner.

"Why am I here?" she demanded and shoved the box she held into his belly, driving the air out of his lungs. At six feet, Joy was bigger than a lot of the men he knew. And twice as strong as they were, too. She stared at him, silently demanding an answer. No one could stare you down like Joy Lovell Peterson. "Was my presence supposed to make her think we're dating?"

"You're married!"

"But she didn't know that. The poor girl

thought she was cutting in on our private time."

He *had* wanted to create a barrier to the attraction he and Sarah felt for each other. But he'd also wanted the person he brought to be a woman—but not so Sarah would mistake that woman as his girlfriend.

"I'm still waiting," Joy said as she tossed the contents of her last box in the recycle bin.

Honestly, did he wear a sign that said, *I'm up to something!* He tried to quickly find an honest answer that wouldn't expose the attraction between Sarah and him as mutual. Joy was an even more deadly matchmaker than his sister Miriam. "I wanted you here so I wouldn't be alone with her. I think she's very lonely and I look unattached. I also knew today would be hard for her. I didn't want to be the one to comfort her because I wouldn't want her to read something into my feelings for her that can never happen. She's a nice lady but I'm not interested in an instant family or a wife. But I still wanted someone here for her emotionally." Which he quickly assured himself was all completely true.

But Joy narrowed those laser blue eyes of hers and continued to stare at him. "Are you saying she's throwing herself at you?"

"No! Sarah would never. She isn't that kind of woman!"

Joy's grin told him he'd fallen into her trap. "And you aren't the least little bit attracted to her?"

Sometimes being a Christian was inconvenient. He couldn't lie. He raked a hand through his hair. "No. I'm plenty attracted," he admitted. "But since I don't want to get married, I don't intend to do anything about it. Letting her think there might be a chance that I'll change my mind would be cruel."

"Kip, you comforted me when Uncle George died. Friends care about each other. You obviously care what happens to her more than just a little."

"But you and I were never attracted to each other. I'm not sure Sarah and I can be *just* friends. But she's lonely and all alone but for her parents who, according to what she told Miriam, worry more about the children at their mission than they do, or ever have, about their own daughter. I'm walking a fine line trying to help without encouraging her feelings. That's all I was trying to do by asking you along."

"Well, you sure accomplished something else on another front altogether. When I let slip that this wasn't a flight arranged by Angel Flight, she about fainted, thinking she should pay for the charter."

Kip frowned. He'd never meant to worry Sarah. But he hadn't wanted to talk to her after the way he'd run from her classroom so he'd decided to have Emily, his secretary, confirm the flight. "I wanted her to know that she didn't owe me anything. I thought it would be easier for her to think this help today had come from the organization and not just the two of us." He put his hand up to stop Joy's rebuttal. "I know I called them on this. But they did help with the fuel costs. So I had Emily call to simply confirm the flight with Sarah and I did make sure she put on her Angel Flight hat for the call."

Joy put her hands on her hips. "Kip, I don't know why you think the Lord has planned a single life for you but I think you're wrong. I don't believe that story that you've had it with women and kids for one second. If you felt that way you wouldn't be a coach, be involved in Angel Flight or worry about Sarah and how she's going to manage."

Kip shrugged and shot her a look that he knew said, *That's my story and I'm stickin' to it.*

Joy all but growled then stalked back to the apartment. He wasn't dumb enough to believe that was the end of the conversation but there was nothing he could do about that now.

It didn't take long to load the truck after that. Unloading it took even less time because they could pull it right up to the cargo ramp. Everything had worked out just the way he'd planned so far.

Once they got to the airport back home, his four brothers-in-law had promised to be there to pack everything into their pickups and then to help heft it all up the narrow wooden stairs to the garage apartment. Then he'd be home free. Sarah would have a great start on a new life and she'd be on her own to build that life.

Without him in it.

At least that was the plan even though it left him feeling oddly empty and sad. He climbed aboard the Convair and pulled the door shut behind him. Joy was there to lock it but then he noticed the cot they always kept onboard for emergencies in case weather grounded the plane overnight in an out-of-the-way place.

Kip frowned. "What's up with the cot?"

"I'm exhausted. You don't really need me

and I'm here if you do. So after takeoff, I intend to catch some Z's. I settled Sarah in the copilot seat. Have a nice flight."

He knew it wasn't over. "You are a rat. You know that?"

Joy grinned. "And you're smitten. You just don't want to admit it. I refuse to help you deny what's right there in front of you." She gave him a jaunty salute and flopped down in her seat. "Now go be a good little fly boy and get us home."

Kip took a breath and trudged up to the cockpit. Sarah sat looking down at the tarmac, obviously terrified. And his heart melted. "Hey," he said, touching her shoulder. The sharp edge of longing for her pierced his heart once again. He ignored it and slid into his seat. "I thought you were only afraid of small planes."

"This is no 747, Kip. But I'm fine about the flight. Don't mind me. I just got a call on my cell phone from Doctor Prentice. He scheduled Grace's surgery. For Monday. It's why we went to Philadelphia, but I'm suddenly panicking. What if it goes all wrong? What if I wasn't supposed to move?"

"It'll be fine. The whole church will be praying and we have some powerful prayer warriors." He was tempted to reach over and give her hand a squeeze but he resisted after that jolt he got when he touched her shoulder. The consequences were too high. "I know the Lord has His hand on Grace," he went on instead and busied himself with the controls. "How else would she have survived so long?"

"I wish I could believe that," she said quietly.

Kip looked at her and saw doubt shadowing her dark eyes. Rather than leap to automatic reassurances, he set about finishing his checklist then got them underway. When he had the flight well under control, he said a quick, fervent prayer for wisdom and the right words.

"Did you really mean that? That you don't think the Lord's hand is on her? She's alive against all the odds. Surely that tells you He's looking out for her."

"Then why was she born so early in the first place? Why couldn't God, *just this once,* have looked at how much I needed her and have made it happen the right way for a change."

"You're talking about your husband's death."

She huffed out an impatient breath. "I'm talking about my whole life!" Tears welled up in her eyes. "Do you know I can hardly remember a birthday spent with my parents? I've spent most of my life feeling like a yo-yo. They'd come and pick me up at a school, then their church would ask them to go somewhere else and they'd find another school to stick me in. Not the one I'd been in but a new one. A new experience, they'd call it. What I called it was more kids who I didn't know and never would. A year would go by and it would happen all over again. It always felt like as soon as I'd really start to fit in, they'd show up and take me with them. I'd get all excited to be with them but it never lasted. Never. I've spent three Christmases with them since I was seven but those were in countries where we couldn't openly celebrate the day.

"They never once saw me graduate from any level of schooling. I begged them to fly home for my wedding. Scott even offered to pay for their plane fare. They said they couldn't possibly see that kind of waste of money for something so foolish. They wanted him to donate the money for the fare to their mission. The point was having them at my wedding, not to gain more money for their flock. I don't even know what he said to them but the dining set arrived from a catalog company a few days before they notified me he'd been killed. I didn't want a gift. I wanted *them.*"

She sniffled. "They didn't come for Scott's funeral, either. Or when Grace was born so early and tiny. Why would a loving God make me grow up on my own like that? Why did he abandon me from the moment I was conceived? Why did my parents abandon me all my life when I've always tried to honor Him and them?"

Kip found his mind was blank. He had no answer. "I don't know," he was forced to admit. "I can see why you feel that way but I just don't have an answer. Maybe you should talk this out with Jim Dillon.

"I can only tell you what I believe and that is that everything in our lives happens for a reason. We just rarely see it while we're in the circumstance. But the Father can use bad things for good and He does it all the time. I really believe that."

Sarah sighed. "I used to believe it too. Maybe because of the way I grew up I was ready to take charge of my life when I lost Scott. But what good can come from him dying before he ever even knew about

Grace? And what good can come of Grace's suffering? What good could either of those things ever bring?"

He sighed. "I wish I knew," he said and shook his head. "But I don't. One day, though, I have a feeling you'll understand why Scott died so young and why Grace was born so early. It'll all make sense to you then, and it'll feel like the sun coming out after a long severe storm. Talk to Jim, Sarah. Don't let bitterness keep you from the Lord's peace," he advised and sent up a quick prayer.

He prayed that God would send someone into Sarah's life to help her move forward and stop looking backward at what might have been.

And this time, he begged, *please, make it someone other than me!*

Chapter Nine

Sarah wasn't sure she could talk with Jim Dillon about this crisis of faith she found herself mired in. She wasn't even sure why she'd blurted out the truth to Kip just now. Maybe because from the moment she'd met him, she'd found Kip easier to talk to than anyone she'd ever known. And because somehow she'd known he wouldn't judge her for her lack of faith.

She was relieved that he'd understood and that he'd been as honest as his pastor had been in that first sermon she'd heard him preach. Kip didn't have an answer for her questions either but at least he hadn't pretended to and spit out meaningless platitudes like an out-of-control change machine.

Sitting there with the drone of the plane's

big engines humming in her ears and the fluffy white clouds drifting by, Sarah almost felt at peace. And she could almost believe all was well with her life.

And with time to think, she now wondered if Kip hadn't actually given her one of the answers she sought. Because of Grace's illness she'd needed the help of Angel Flight East. And she'd moved away from a community where she hadn't ever really belonged. Kip had helped her find a charming affordable apartment in a lovely area along with a wonderful job she already loved. Because of Kip and Joy she would have all her furniture and had been able to bring along more of her own belongings than she'd dared hope.

And Monday morning, Grace would have a life-saving surgery done by a world-renowned surgeon. After that it would be clear sailing for her. Grace would gain more weight and finally come home to be with her. So maybe all that was evidence that God was working in her life and using what seemed like a bad thing for the good.

If Grace made it through the surgery, maybe some of this nightmare *would* make sense. Still, it hardly seemed fair to a tiny baby to be forced to begin life with such an uphill battle to fight just so her mother lived and worked where God, for some unknown reason, wanted her.

Frustrated, Sarah stared out the cockpit window at God's vast creation, determined to pray for her child. But though she said the words, begging God's blessing on Dr. Prentice and, of course, on Grace, she felt none of the peace that prayer had once given her. The sad truth was she had once believed He listened, but now Sarah just wasn't sure.

Several hours later, Sarah walked back out of her bedroom and looked around her apartment. It was perfect. Exactly the way she'd pictured it before she'd gotten practical and began editing out the larger pieces of her furniture as not feasible to move.

"This is the last of it," Kip said as he came in with a second item she was reluctant to set up. Grace's crib. It was still in its box like the matching combination dresser and dressing table had been before Miriam and her husband Gary insisted they put it together. She could hear them behind her, kibitzing over which pieces needed assembling next.

"Just lean it there. I'll drag it into the bedroom later," she told him.

Kip leaned away from the box a little and looked at the picture on the front. "Why don't we put it together? Then you'll have it ready and be able to visualize her where she belongs."

She bit her lip, unsure. She really hadn't wanted to set up either of the pieces until Grace was ready to come home.

"Sarah," Kip said gently, "there's no such thing as tempting fate. There's no such thing as fate, bad luck or good luck. There's just life. And God's grace to get us through it."

She huffed out a breath. "I know. I guess I'm just anxious about Monday."

"What happens Monday?" Miriam asked from the doorway of the bedroom.

Sarah turned. "Oh, I'm sorry. With all the hubbub over getting all this moved up here I forgot to tell you. Dr. Prentice called my cell phone just before we took off for home. He's scheduled Grace's surgery for Monday."

"That's wonderful. It means our girl's getting stronger!" Miriam exclaimed, but Sarah guessed some of her anxiety must have shown because Miriam's smile faded. "Now, Sarah, it's going to be all right. I just know it is. Still, you shouldn't go through this alone. The problem is, I can't take off if you do. That would mean finding two subs for the day and our list of available subs is pretty short right now."

"Don't worry about it. I'll be fine. I've been doing things on my own a long time. I'm used to it."

Miriam frowned. "Well, you shouldn't have to be. Pastor Jim leaves tomorrow afternoon for the East Coast Pastors' Conference. Suppose I give one of his assistant pastors a call."

Over the years Sarah had learned that the only thing worse than doing things on her own was doing them with the support of strangers. It always made her feel awkward and more lonely than just alone. "I'd rather you didn't. I don't really know any of them."

Miriam's worried frown suddenly changed back to a smile when she looked over at Kip who'd begun opening the crib's packaging. "Kip, why don't you take off and wait with Sarah?"

"Miriam, Kip probably has work," Sarah protested.

Miriam propped her hands on her narrow hips. "Nonsense. There's no point in being a partner in a business if you can't make your own hours."

Sarah's cheeks felt as if they'd caught fire when Kip glared at his sister in obvious displeasure. She whirled to face Miriam again. "Kip's done more than enough, Miriam. I told you, I'm used to being on my own. I'll be fine." She nearly said she preferred it that way but that would be a bald-faced lie. She *could* do it. Had *done* it all her life but the truth was she was sick to death of going it alone.

"No. It's fine, Sarah," she heard Kip say behind her. She pivoted to face him, surprised to find him looking at her with tenderness. "I'd really like to be there. What time did Prentice say you needed to get there? Six was the time of the surgery, right?"

She nodded. "About five or five-thirty. But really, you don't need to do this."

"Sarah, public transportation doesn't start up till five. The train doesn't get to our station till six and you need to be in the city before that. I'll pick you up at quarter to five. That way, you can have lots of time with her before surgery."

"Kip, are you sure? I could stay downtown tomorrow night. I don't want you doing this because your sister embarrassed you into it."

He grinned. "I haven't let my sister embarrass me into doing anything since the first grade."

"Oh, not this again," Miriam all but wailed.

Kip grinned. "Ah ah ah. We'll let Sarah judge," Kip said, the smile in his voice making it plain that he enjoyed teasing his sister. "You see, I asked for a superhero lunchbox and Mom bought me one but it was a *girl* hero. Miriam talked me into carrying it so I wouldn't hurt Mom's feelings. I *never* lived it down."

Caught up in the sibling banter, Sarah crossed her arms and leaned against the back of the sofa pretending to consider Kip's childhood plight. She looked from one to the other then shook her head. "Miriam, for shame."

Kip bowed comically. "I thank you, my lady." Then he pointed at his sister. "Judged guilty by the fair Sarah."

"I've been telling her for years it's fear of getting a woman like one of his sisters that keeps the man single," Gray shouted from the bedroom. "Kip, drag that crib on in here and we'll get it set up. Shouldn't those pizzas you two ordered be ready about now, *darling*."

"Don't *darling* me, you traitor," Miriam retorted over her shoulder. "And, yes, they should be. Sarah, are you sure you want to feed all of these guys? A moving van may have been cheaper."

Sarah smiled and sighed happily. Kip was so lucky. He had the nicest family. "I'm very sure," she said and went to find her purse.

Monday dawned rainy and cold, making Sarah more than simply grateful for the lift into the city. She already stood waiting for Kip under the overhang at the front of the garage when he pulled in. When she climbed into the passenger seat and sat next to him, Kip handed her a coffee. "Heavy on the cream and light on the sugar," he told her.

Though he was careful not to let their fingers touch, he'd still remembered her preference. The thought warmed her though she told herself it meant nothing. Kip was just a nice man. A friend. Nothing more.

"Oh, bless you," she said and took a sip of the sharp creamy brew. "I swear I'm chilled to the bone."

"What are you going to do when winter gets here, on the twenty-second, woman?" Kip teased with a lazy half smile.

"If it's this cold, I'm going to shake and shiver like I did last year, but I'll love every minute of it. Last winter I arrived straight from Doctal in the middle of a snowstorm. What an initiation back into the States! I loved it. Will we get a lot here?"

Kip shrugged. "Some winters it seems to snow a few inches once a week just to be annoying. Then other winters we get socked with a couple of big ones. Those pretty much shut everything down for a few hours—at most a day. Those are the fun ones. It winds up that everyone has extra time on their hands because they can't go anywhere. But that makes time for snowball fights. Building snowmen. And sledding. If I know one's going to hit, I try to stay at one of my sisters' houses and borrow the kids for a few hours." He laughed. "An adult just can't play in the snow without kids along or we look demented!"

Sarah nodded and smiled but inside she was heartily confused. She sipped her coffee and slid a sideways glance at Kip. According to Miriam, he said marriage and kids weren't for him. That he was sick of them and women because he'd grown up in a house overflowing with both. But he couldn't seem to turn down an appeal for help involving them either. If he wasn't ferrying a sick child to a needed hospital, he was coaching a team, mentoring a troubled boy or babysitting for his nieces and nephews.

It made no sense.

She and Kip arrived at the hospital by five and rushed up to the neonatal intensive care unit so she could squeeze in every last minute with Grace. At the entrance to the scrubbing room Sarah stopped when Kip said, "I'll meet you in the green room. I think it's down the hall and around the corner."

The thought struck her that Kip should spend time with Grace, too. She wouldn't be at CHOP at all were it not for his generosity. "Do you want to come in with me?"

Kip smiled. "Yeah, if it's allowed. She sort of stole my heart the day I flew her here."

"I noticed," Sarah told him and smiled, too, in spite of her nerves. The first of the nurses she'd met, Leslie Washington, was back with Grace. Sarah knocked on the window and motioned to Kip. Leslie nodded her permission with a wide smile.

They scrubbed up, donned the sterile gowns and made their way to Grace's corner of the NICU. Just as before, Kip didn't look at her child with horror but with wonder as he bent over Grace. "I can't believe how tiny she is yet every part of her is so perfectly formed already. Look at those tiny nails! And I swear she's gained weight!"

"She was two pounds this morning," Grace's nurse, Leslie said. "She's doing so good!"

"You hear that, Amazing Gracie," Kip said, making Sarah smile at the nickname that just seemed to pop out of his mouth. "You'll be home in your own pretty crib before you know it. This time next year your mama's going to have her hands full with you cruising all over the place."

"From your lips to God's ears," Leslie said. "You know, I have an idea." She pursed her lips. "You wait right there," she ordered then rushed away. A few minutes later she was back and as she approached them she grabbed a rocking chair. "Sit, mama. It's time you held this baby of yours."

Terror struck Sarah's heart. Because of the ventilator she'd never been allowed to hold Grace. Was she being given this opportunity because Leslie thought after surgery it might be too late because Grace would be gone? But she sat, not wanting to put Leslie in the position of saying something so difficult. Leslie lifted Grace from the warming bed and settled her on Sarah's thighs. She covered her and left them alone for a little while.

It seemed only minutes had gone by when she returned to say it was time for Grace to be prepped for surgery. She let Sarah continue to hold her while she took off the ever-present cap and booties that helped her retain warmth. "Okay. We need to go now," she said, clearly understanding how difficult this was.

Kip nodded. "Mind if I pray for her?" he asked. "I promise to keep it short."

Sarah blinked back tears as her throat closed up, dreading the moment she would hand her child over for surgery. And she didn't know what to say to Kip. Would God listen to his prayers when He always seemed to turn a deaf ear to hers? She rubbed fingertips over Grace's downy hair. It was worth a try. There was everything to gain.

"Please," she whispered, looking up at him as she held her precious baby cradled on her lap. "Maybe He'll listen to you."

Kip could hear Sarah's doubt and her desperation. He went down on one knee and he cupped his hand carefully around Grace's head where it rested just above Sarah's knees. Leslie Washington must have heard the quiet desperation in Sarah's voice because her hand moved to Sarah's shoulder and her other covered Grace's chest.

"So so tiny, you are," he whispered to Grace. "But so amazingly made. We place her in the palm of Your hand, Lord Jesus. Her mother and I pray You will guide Doctor Prentice's skilled hands and the hands and minds of all those involved today. We beg Your intercession so that she'll prosper and grow into a healthy little girl, continuing to be the joy of her mama's world and a testament to Your greatness. Amen."

"And Amen!" Leslie added with the kind of enthusiasm only a believer could have over a prayer.

Kip looked up at Sarah and saw a little more confidence creep into her soft dark eyes. He truly believed Grace would prosper and grow. He didn't know why he believed it so strongly when to all indications she shouldn't even be alive. But he did.

Sarah reluctantly handed Grace into the waiting hands of her nurse. Kip didn't think he'd ever get over the sight of her sitting for a long moment in that old rocking chair, her arms still extended as the nurse turned and walked away with Grace. The longing and fear in Sarah's eyes nearly broke his heart.

In many ways, he was glad Miriam had forced him to do what he'd wanted to do anyway. But it was a worry to him just how much he'd wanted to be there for Sarah. She meant too much to him and after today he'd have to find more ways to steer clear of her.

It seemed like it was the only way to handle the problem. He couldn't be sure though because at the ripe old age of thirty-two he'd never before encountered a woman who made him feel the way Sarah did. Remaining uninvolved had never been a challenge before.

But then one day he'd found Sarah staring at his plane in sheer terror and determination. Until that moment no woman had ever caused even a ripple of anxiety in his heart over the thought of her sharing her life with another man. He felt like an idiot praying for the thing he dreaded most—that a man to love them would walk into Sarah and Grace's lives.

There was no one in the green room when they got there except a volunteer who offered them coffee and donuts. Sarah shook her head and went to perch on the wide sill of a window that looked out over the university campus. A couple came in a few minutes later chatting as if they hadn't a care in the world. It was a little annoying but Sarah didn't seem to notice. She just stared out across the campus as if engrossed. An hour later Sarah hadn't moved.

Then the phone rang and she jolted to her feet and pivoted toward the elderly volunteer at the desk. Kip knew it was too soon to be news about Grace. Leslie had said it might be at least two hours or maybe even longer before they heard anything. The volunteer called the other couple's name. They stood, listened to a report on the minor surgery their child had had, then they sailed out.

Sarah watched them leave, then she paced to the hall and back to the window. She might have paced for the next hour but he turned a page in the magazine he'd been thumbing through and found an article on an Internet company that sold clothes appropriate for preemies and what they called micro preemies who were living their first months in a NICU. Micro sounded like a perfect description of Grace.

"Hey, Sarah, look at this article."

"What's it about?" she asked and sat in the

chair next to him. Her voice had held a desperate edge as if she were as eager for a distraction as he was to provide one.

"It's about a grandmother who started a company after her daughter had a baby who was just a little bigger than Grace was. They make clothes designed for the tender skin of preemies in a lot of different prints and colors. There are long and short-sleeve T-shirts and something called a body tee that covers their diaper too. And they used her grandson's measurements as he grew to work out better sizing than other manufacturers have."

Sarah's eyes lit up. "You mean I could buy her something to wear?" she asked and held her hands out for the magazine.

"Looks like," he said and handed it to her, silently thanking God for providing the perfect distraction.

Time moved forward after that but as hour two moved into three they were both wired. Sarah had devoured several parenting magazines but abandoned reading for pacing again. He turned and bumped into her. Only then did he realize he'd been pacing for a few minutes himself.

"What's taking so long?" she demanded, her eyes full of frustration and fear.

He settled his hands on her shoulders. "Take a deep breath. Leslie only said how long the surgery itself would take. We don't know if Prentice started at six or not. Prep and anesthesia may have taken longer than we think." He forced a smile. "He could have had a flat tire on the expressway."

"If we don't hear something soon I'll go stark raving—"

Sarah didn't finish her thought because the phone on the volunteer's desk rang. They both turned as one, hanging on every nod, every syllable the woman uttered.

"Fine. I'll tell them," she said and hung up.

"You can relax, you two. Doctor Prentice will be down to talk to you in a little while. Your baby came through the surgery just fine." She stood. "I'll be back."

Kip looked back at Sarah and she looked up at him, a broad, relieved smile tipping the corners of her exquisite lips. He didn't know what made him lean down and capture those lips with his own. He was sure he meant it as a celebration but what flared between them was more—and dangerous. Still holding her shoulders, Kip stepped back and all but thrust her away.

He felt singed. Branded. And terrified.

They were connected. Not just through Grace. But through feelings he very much feared he had no control over. And worse, at that moment, the connection felt unbreakable.

Suddenly and without warning Kip understood and found he shared some of Sarah's doubts about the way God operated in the lives of His people.

Why now?

Why, when he had less than a decade left to live, would he suddenly be shown heaven on earth and know he had to find a way to push it forever out of reach?

Chapter Ten

Sarah stood staring up at Kip, her head in a whirl, taken from the heights to the depths in seconds. He'd kissed her. She'd thought in celebration but in a nanosecond her mind and senses had filled with feelings that were all about him and not about Grace at all. The strength of the longing she'd felt was like nothing she'd ever experienced before. She felt as if a flame had just sparked to life in a part of her she hadn't even known existed. It was a part of her that Scott had never come close to touching.

And then just as she'd recovered from the shock of the effect of his warm lips on hers and his strong arms holding her so close, Kip had suddenly pushed her away as if she were poison. And the look in his eyes said he saw her as exactly that.

She looked away and sank into the chair next to her purse, tears burning at the back of her eyes. It was the same as that day in her art room. Once again Kip apparently wanted to be anywhere but near her. Had she misunderstood his meaning and responded in a way he hadn't expected or wanted?

No matter.

Right then she wanted him gone as much as he apparently wanted to go. Sarah felt a blush start to heat her face and cast about on the floor next to her for her purse. She grabbed it, and started looking through it, searching for something—anything to divert attention from what had just happened between them. Meanwhile Kip turned away and walked to the windows.

Blessedly her hand fell on her pack of tissues. "Thanks again for waiting with me," she managed to choke out as she made a production of sniffling and dabbing at tears. Rather than being from relief for Grace's safe deliverance through surgery, they were tears of heartache. But she had to make him think it was only Grace on her mind. Her pride would consider nothing else.

Because, against all odds, she'd begun to fall in love with the knight who'd flown to her rescue time and time again. It hadn't happened because of the rescues, though, but because of the genuinely kind, fascinating and attractive man that Kip had turned out to be. Again that small piece of her conversation during her interview with Jim came to mind. When she looked at Kip she felt none of the doubts about her feelings that had assailed her with Scott. The only doubt rested in his feelings for her.

"Waiting with you was no problem, Sarah," Kip assured her. "Look, I'm sorry if I just gave you the wrong idea."

Which meant her reaction to his kissing her *was* the problem. More exactly her *feelings* were the problem. No shock there at least. As she forced herself to look up at him, wearing a wry smile she'd pasted on her still tingling lips, Sarah hoped those drama classes in boarding school had taught her something.

"What wrong idea?" she tried to feign confusion, then said, "Goodness, Kip. Do you mean because you kissed me? I've been married. I'm not about to blow one little kiss out of proportion. I'm not some starry-eyed child."

He nodded. "Good. That's good. I really like you, Sarah, but I know you aren't the type of woman interested in anything temporary. You have permanent written all over you."

"Thank you for that, I think," she said, not sure if to Kip that was a good thing or not. "I know from your sister you aren't interested in marriage but I hadn't thought you were the kind of man who sought out the fringe benefits of it without the commitment."

Kip had the good grace to look embarrassed. "I don't. That's why I'm trying to warn you. I don't want to see you hurt. I'm really only a friendship kind of guy. I like my freedom but I love my Lord. So…"

"I get it. Okay. Just friends. So, thanks for waiting with me and distracting me but I told both you and Miriam that I could have done this on my own. I'm very capable when I need to be."

"According to what you said on Saturday, you've always *needed* to be. And you didn't sound thrilled about it. Miriam was right. You shouldn't have had to wait alone."

"And thanks to you I didn't. Thank you for your company. Now you can go off to work with a clear conscience. I'm staying for the rest of the day, though. So you may as well leave."

"You're sure?"

"I wouldn't have said it if I didn't mean it. Grace and I will muddle along just fine by ourselves."

Kip nodded. "All right then." He backed away toward the hall. "Give Grace a kiss for me." Now he stood uncertainly in the doorway. His eyes looked tortured. Clearly he was still worried that he'd hurt her feelings. "And…I'm glad it turned out okay for her. For you…uh…both," he stammered, then he was gone. Running again just as he had before.

Sarah breathed a sigh of relief even as she mopped up more tears. She felt like a fool. A lonely fool who'd fallen for the first guy who was nice to her.

To Sarah it seemed that God was paying her back for promising to love and honor someone when she apparently hadn't had a clue what real love felt like. She'd liked Scott a lot. Had even loved him in some ways. But now she was sure she hadn't been *in* love with him. She'd felt only half for Scott what she did already for Kip.

Wasn't losing Scott before even getting a chance to prove herself worthy of his love enough punishment? Did God have to be so cruel as to put Kip, an even more spectacular man, in her life only to yank him away just when she'd realized she loved him?

It sounded just like the God her last pastor had preached about and even more like what she'd heard in various schools she'd attended over the years. It didn't sound like Pastor Dillon's version of God, though. Or Kip's. But they had to be wrong because that was exactly what had happened. The door to having a real full family life and belonging to someone special had once again slammed shut in her face.

From that moment on, Sarah swore Grace's happiness would be her focus.

Her only focus.

Grace was all Sarah would ever let herself care about. They would be enough family for each other.

The phone woke Sarah from a sound sleep in the middle of the night between Thursday and Friday a week and a half later. She was in an exhausted stupor because Grace had been uncharacteristically fussy the night before so Sarah had stayed at the hospital till minutes before the last train pulled out of 30th Street Station around one in the morning.

The utter darkness of the moonless night disoriented her further. She groped around on the nightstand, reaching for the clanging instrument of her torture.

"Hello," she rasped when she got the receiver to her ear.

"Mrs. Bates. This is Angela, Grace's night nurse."

Alarm spread through Sarah and shot her upright in an instant. "What is it? What's wrong?"

"Grace began running a fever. There's no reason to think she's in immediate danger but the doctor thought you should be alerted to the change in her condition. You don't need to rush down here—"

Not in immediate danger. But didn't that mean there was danger on the way? And it was a change in her condition. From doing just fine to what? "I'll be there as soon as I can," she promised as she popped to her feet, not waiting for another ridiculous suggestion that Grace didn't need her. A baby needed her mother when she was sick. And a mother certainly needed to be with her baby at a time like that too. At least this mother did!

She picked up her alarm clock and stared at it. Three-oh-two. How was she going to get there now? She still didn't have her car. That was days away. She hated to wait for the first train into the city. It wouldn't get to her stop till six. She just couldn't wait that long!

Sarah could hardly call Miriam and risk waking all five of her children. Besides, Gary was out of town which meant Miriam couldn't drive her unless she woke her kids, dragged them out of bed and to the car for the long ride into the city. And she'd need the car to get them all to Tabernacle Christian in the morning which meant Sarah couldn't just borrow it. Miriam, like Kip, had done enough for her but, once again, he was the only one she could turn to.

She stalked to the phone and dialed Kip's number before she could chicken out and change her mind. In a way, asking his help was a good thing, she told herself. They'd chatted amiably when they'd run into one another at school. He'd even stopped by her classroom to say hello and check on his nieces' and nephews' artwork. She'd teased him unmercifully about some of the depictions of him while loving him under the guise of friend.

But calling him for help would go even further toward convincing him she'd thought nothing of that incredible, monumental moment when he'd kissed her. His phone rang. And rang. She listened hoping he'd answer after the message machine picked up.

"You've reached my machine because I'm not available. You know what to do when you hear the beep. Catch you later. Bye."

Momentarily mesmerized by the sound of his slightly baritone voice, the beep took Sarah by surprise. "Kip, um…this is Sarah. I guess you aren't there. I needed a ride. It's okay, though. I'll figure something out."

She hung up, not even sure what she'd said. Her mind had already moved on to finding a way into the city in the middle of the night. If she was in the city she'd take a cab. That was it! She'd call a cab. She hadn't seen any in the area but there had to be a cab company. She found a listing for CCCC— Chester County Cab Company—right away.

It took an hour and frankly her entire food budget for the week but she arrived at CHOP, signed in with the guard in the lobby by four-fifteen and rushed to the NICU.

Grace had more than a slight fever by the time she arrived. Somehow even with all the precautions they took as a matter of routine, Grace had pneumonia. Sarah found herself agreeing to anything Doctor Prentice and Doctor Kelly suggested, even returning her to the respirator she'd been off since her surgery.

Minutes dragged into hours. Any ground Grace had picked up in the last week and a half, she lost. The hours slid from dawn, to morning and onto afternoon, evening then back to night. And fever still ravaged Grace's tiny body. How much could one little baby take? Doctor Kelly had been brutally honest only minutes before. Not much more.

They all insisted Sarah go to the cafeteria for meals to keep up her strength. She obeyed by rote. Bought food because she had to and ate it but she never did remember what it was she'd eaten when she got back upstairs.

As she rushed down the hall after an equally forgettable dinner, Sarah heard her name called from behind her just as she reached the NICU.

She stopped and turned toward the frantic voice. "Miriam, what on earth are you doing here? Did Kip tell you about Grace?"

"Kip? I haven't talked to him. I've been calling him on and off all day to see if he knew what had happened to you. We never connected. Honestly this medical privacy stuff is more trouble than it's worth. They wouldn't tell me a thing. Not even if you were here or not. Sarah, no one knew where you were. You didn't call in to school or get a sub for your classes."

Sarah felt as if her brain had just overloaded. She sank down on a hall bench and blinked away tears that threatened her precarious composure—or was all her composure just plain exhausted numbness? She had no idea.

"Then Gary's car wouldn't start at the airport," Miriam went on, "let's just say it was a crazy day or I'd have been here sooner."

"Am I fired?" Sarah asked, noting the hollow sound of her own voice. At that point she didn't think she cared. Living there, working there, fixing up the apartment had all been about Grace and providing her the best life possible. Now hope seemed to be dwindling that Grace would survive the coming night.

Miriam's eyes widened. She opened her

mouth, closed it then shook her head. "Fired? Of course not. We all figured something had gone wrong with Grace. We were all just frantic to know what. What's going on, honey?"

"She has pneumonia," she said, her voice cracking. "I'm so scared."

"Why didn't you call me?"

"They called around three in the morning. I couldn't wake you and the kids. Kip didn't answer at his place but I calmed down after I left him a message. I realized there must be a cab company so I found one in the phone book. They came and got me and I've been here since."

"You called Kip and he never called us or came here to make sure you were all right? I'll kill him!"

In her entire life Sarah didn't remember ever losing her temper but anger surged through her. "I'd rather you just stay out of it! He doesn't care about me other than as a charity case. At best I'm a buddy. And I can't tell you how *flattering* that is. The poor man must be sick to death of having you push me and my problems on him when he wants nothing to do with me. Losing Scott was bad enough. I still may lose Grace and now I've lost Kip when I never really had a chance with him. News flash! He's *not* interested in me."

Miriam's face flamed with obvious chagrin. "Oh, Sarah. I'm so terribly sorry." She reached out and put her hand on Sarah's shoulder. "I-I never meant to hurt you. I've been selfish, only thinking of Kip."

Sarah took a deep breath and got hold of the temper she hadn't even known she had. But, right then, she really didn't want Miriam's comfort. She stood and walked a few steps away before turning back. "I'm sorry I shouted at you but, Miriam, Kip is a big boy. He doesn't need you trying to run his life. Maybe *Kip* knows what *Kip* needs and wants. At any rate, whatever that is, I can tell you, it isn't me."

"Oh, Sarah, but it *is*. I see the way he looks at you."

"Are you sure that isn't wishful thinking on your part?"

Miriam shook her head. "I also see the way he looks at my sisters and me when we're with our husbands. He looks sad and lonely. He fills his empty hours with any and all activities so he doesn't have to be alone. He needs the exact thing he's avoiding—a wife and children of his own. I'm so afraid he'll get to a place in his life where it's too late and he realizes he's made a mistake."

"It's his mistake to make. He's made it perfectly plain that regardless of any feelings I have for him, he's not interested. I hope I've managed to convince him that I never thought of him as more than a friend. Leave me a little pride. Please, just leave me out of your dreams for your brother. Those are *your* dreams—not his."

Miriam nodded. "I *am* sorry. I never meant to hurt you. I'm sure Kip never did either."

"Look, I'm sorry I exploded like that."

"It's okay. Your emotions are in a tangle with Grace so ill. I understand. I just wish I could stay with you tonight but, as I said, Gary leaves again in the morning. I have to get home."

Sarah shook her head. "You have a family to take care of. I'll be fine on my own," she repeated for yet another audience, knowing she'd just have to get used to going it alone all over again.

Chapter Eleven

Kip landed the King Air 440 on the slick runway and brought the plane to a careful stop. He breathed a sigh of relief and yanked off his headset.

What a flight!

Yawning, he squeezed the back of his neck and started his post-flight check by rote. Minutes later when he pushed open the hatch, cold rain and ice pellets slashed his face. He ducked his head and ran for the door to Agape Air's hanger.

Once inside he stopped and leaned against the wall, inhaling the smell of fuel, oil and steel. He was tempted to tinker with the engine on the WWII fighter he and Joy had been rebuilding for air shows but he knew he was too tired.

Besides, he had to deal with the knowledge that he should have canceled the flight earlier that afternoon or at least stayed the night in Maryland. It just wasn't like him to take off with an iffy weather report. Safety always came first.

But then a lot of things he'd been doing lately weren't like him. He just couldn't seem to stop himself from pushing ahead with a dogged determination bordering on irrationality toward any and all activities. And he knew if he didn't deal with the demons driving him, someone was going to get hurt. He'd prayed endlessly for peace but none came his way. The only time he was able to get Sarah out of his head was while flying. When he was at the school, he couldn't seem to stay away from her. He sought her out for news of Grace just so he could look at her and with his coaching obligations he had to be at the school as often as he could arrange it around his schedule.

He stood and yawned. There was an old sofa in his office that had his name on it. There was nothing he could do about the situation with Sarah so he pushed onward as he had been, promising himself that next time he'd think twice before acting on any ideas that included hundreds of gallons of fuel and being thousands of feet in the air.

Once inside Agape Air's public space, Kip noticed light pouring into the hall from Joy's office. It was very unusual that late at night for Joy to be anywhere but home with her doctor husband. At the open door of her office, Kip tapped his knuckle on the door frame. "Burning the midnight oil?" he asked as he poked his head into his partner's office.

"There was a pileup on I-95. Brian's still in surgery patching up the damage a skidding tractor trailer did to three kids. I decided until he was ready to head home, I'd try catching up on paperwork and rearrange the flight schedule for the next few days. I had to cancel three flights after you took off. It should have been four," she said pointedly with a raised eyebrow.

Kip leaned a shoulder against the door-jamb. She could wait all night for an explanation because he wasn't volunteering one. He held up his hand. "I hear you. And, for what it's worth, I know you're right."

She stared at him for a long moment then sighed. "So stand down tomorrow."

"We'll see." And that was all the concession he would give. "You complaining about the profit the extra flights have brought in?"

Joy leaned back in her chair and crossed her arms. "You're going to make me ask, aren't you? What's up with you? You're hiding in your work and have been for a couple of weeks."

Kip just stared and crossed his arms, too.

"Fine," Joy huffed out. "Just please, whatever the problem is," she said with a smile in her voice. "Don't take it out on our new five point three million-dollar aircraft again. It plays merry havoc with our insurance premiums when someone bends the equipment."

"Your precious King Air is all in one piece. And for the record, you're the only one in the room who's ever bent the equipment."

Still defensive about the crash she'd been in while on a search-and-rescue mission, Joy rolled her eyes at his tease. "Lightning bent the equipment—not me. But fine, we'll change the subject. You have a few messages on your desk you can handle when you get in tomorrow but there's one from your sister, Miriam, I wouldn't put off. You're supposed to call her."

Kip yawned and looked at his watch. "I'll get to her in the morning, too."

Joy shook her head. "She said no matter

what time you got in. She sounded pretty adamant."

He sighed and squeezed the muscle knot in his neck again. "As only Miriam can. Okay, I'll call her from my office so you don't get on her wrong side."

"Good boy," Joy said and grinned.

"Are you as big a pain in the neck for your brother as she is for me?"

She laughed. "Worse. I'm something you don't have. I'm a dreaded *younger* sister."

"Oh please. Younger cousins were enough torture," he told her and chuckled. Then he waved and strode into his office. After turning on his desk lamp he stripped out of his WWII bomber jacket and tossed it on the old sofa. He looked longingly at the sofa. He just might sleep there considering how tired he was and what road conditions must be like. He punched in Miriam's number as he sank into his chair. She surprised him by answering on the first ring.

"Were you sitting on top of the phone?" he asked as he put his feet on the desk and propped the phone on his shoulder.

"Actually, I was. Don't you answer your cell phone anymore?" she demanded sounding completely out of patience.

Kip chuckled. "The kids must have been in rare form for you to sound this cranky. Forgot to charge my cell. I was in a plane. My charger's in my car and—"

"Kip! Tell me you didn't just land in this!"

Enough with everyone telling him what he already knew. "I didn't have much choice other than running out of gas in the air," he snapped.

He heard her take a deep breath as if she was reaching for patience. That made two of them.

"I've been trying to reach you for a good reason," she told him.

So fine, he'd give her his complete itinerary for the last two days. That ought to get her off his back. "Hey, sis, I have a company to help run, remember? I've been busy. I didn't get home last night till after three, slept till noon, took off at three and just got back."

"You should still take time to listen to your personal messages when you're home."

He sighed. What was her problem? "Like which one?" he asked and knew he sounded exasperated.

"The one from *Sarah*."

Kip closed his eyes. He'd heard it all right. And he'd erased it when he'd caught himself listening to it for the third time just to hear the sound of her voice. He'd managed to avoid her for the last two days by staying away from the school and having Jim handle his practices. But he missed her so much that a casual message had thrown him into a state where he'd taken a flight that afternoon that he should have refused.

"I got her message. She said she needed a lift. It must have been earlier in the afternoon when I was in Pittsburgh waiting for a customer. I told you, I got home at three-fifteen or three-thirty in the morning. I could hardly call her then."

"She didn't leave the message at three *P.M.* It was three in the morning when she called. She must have barely missed you. She needed to get to the hospital because the NICU called to tell her Grace is sick."

His heart fell. "Sick?"

"Oh, Kip." Miriam sniffled. "They aren't even sure that sweet baby's going to make it through the night."

Kip dropped his feet to the floor, stunned. The blood drained from his head. *"What?"*

"She has pneumonia."

Kip closed his eyes. Sarah couldn't lose Grace now. *Please, Lord, no,* he prayed silently but only because he couldn't seem to make an intelligible sound.

"I went to CHOP to find out what was going on because no one at school had heard from her. And then I came home to a house full of sick kids otherwise I'd have gone back once they were all settled in bed," Miriam went on. "Gary took them to a buffet while I tracked Sarah down. Something they all ate, including Gary, has had them sick as dogs. Things are quieting down but I still can't leave them. I feel terrible about Sarah. We befriended her and now we've left her to go through this alone. I know you've had a long day but, sweetie, is there any way you can get to the hospital?"

"I'm on my way," he managed to say. "Pray, Mir. If Sarah loses that baby now, she's never going to get over it."

Emotionally or spiritually.

Kip asked for Joy's prayers, too, before hot-footing it into the city. The slick roads made the trip nearly as treacherous as his landing had been but he couldn't have stayed away. He did the same thing now he'd done when his wings had started picking up ice.

He prayed.

But not for a safe landing this time. He prayed for Grace. He prayed for Sarah.

Sarah.

Sweet. Gentle. Brave, Sarah.

He wasn't even sure she'd want to see him. She'd put on a good act that day he'd kissed her but he'd seen through the bravado to the hurt he knew he'd inflicted. If only that spontaneous kiss hadn't been so amazingly frightening. He just hadn't been ready to feel all those emotions, especially not that soul-deep yearning to have her in his arms forever.

He'd been completely unprepared because he hadn't even suspected it could happen to him. After all, it never had before.

And because of that, he'd hurt Sarah even though he hadn't meant to. He'd actually been trying to *keep* from hurting her. He hoped she realized that. He thought she did considering how friendly she was whenever they saw each other since that day.

He only hoped his going to the hospital tonight didn't open her up to more hurt. It might not be fair to encourage her to lean on him again after what had happened. But, as Miriam said, it wasn't right to let her sit alone to possibly watch her child die, either. There was no perfect answer to his dilemma but erring on the side of compassion instead of caution felt right.

Kip shook his head as he pulled into the underground parking garage. He couldn't even wrap his head around Amazing Gracie not making it. She'd fought so hard. Overcome so much.

She had to keep fighting, he thought as he pushed open the door to the hospital. And he'd tell her that if he got to see her.

In the lobby the guard knew him and so he waved him toward the bank of elevators after he'd scribbled his name on the sign-in sheet and explained why he was there. A few pushed buttons later, he exited the elevator car and saw Sarah. She sat alone on a bench outside the NICU hugging herself.

She looked up when he got close, her face a frozen mask. "She shouldn't have bothered you. I told her to leave you out of this."

Kip sat next to her, leaned his elbows on his thighs and clasped his hands. "Since when does Miriam listen to anyone? And in this case, I'm glad she didn't. I want to be here. For Grace and for you. This is another wait you shouldn't have to do alone. The kids and Gary are down with some sort of food poisoning or she'd be here with me. That's what friends do for each other."

They sat in tense silence for several minutes. "Are you allowed in with Grace?"

She sighed lightly and nodded. "A little. Doctor Kelly and some new lung doctor are in with her now. I can go in again when they're done. We had to put her back on the respirator instead of the c-pap that she'd graduated to after surgery. She was doing so well."

"And she'll do just as good again. It's just a little set back."

Sarah sat back and leaned against the wall but he could see her out of the corner of his eye. The more relaxed posture meant nothing. "You must get a lot of practice at lying? You're pretty good at it."

He should have been insulted because he'd always tried not to lie but he supposed leading everyone to believe he *preferred* a life alone was a lie in many ways. In truth, he'd become discontented with his life over the last couple of years and more so since meeting Sarah. In her, he saw the true depth of what he was missing.

The discontent had begun because in those last two years he'd helped straighten out a few boys in partnership with Jim Dillon. One was bitter and acting out against teachers and his mother because he'd lost his father through divorce and a long distance move.

Another lost his dad through death as Kip had lost his own father. He'd been taking on too much responsibility for his younger brothers and sisters and household chores and his grades were failing. His father had inadvertently set up the reaction because he'd told him he'd be the man of the family when he was gone.

The third kid had a complete set of very nice blue-collar parents who were bewildered by a superintelligent child they had nothing in common with. To make matters worse, his IQ set him apart in school because most kids saw him as different.

Once the boys were on the right track, Kip's interaction with them always lessened as it was supposed to. Moving on, though, had left him knowing more about what he was missing by not having his own kids. The life he'd chosen left him feeling like a kid himself—one with his nose pressed to the window of a store he couldn't afford to enter even though inside was his heart's desire.

Even with his own family, Kip was always on the outside looking in at them. A guest. Well loved but still just a guest.

But it was Sarah who'd shown him that what he was really missing was completion. She would complete him. Sitting right next to her, feeling her fear and pain yet knowing he could do only just so much to help was torture.

Not for the first time, he wished his aunt had left him as blissfully ignorant of the full truth about his father's death as his mother had wanted him to be. Aunt Emily had told him they'd disagreed on the subject. He knew she must have felt very strongly that it was the right thing to do. Because somehow Aunt Emily found the courage to go against his mom when she'd never had the strength to function on her own in any other way. The two women had relied so heavily on each other that Kip had kept quiet, not wanting to upset the delicate balance of the household. And also because he hadn't wanted endless dissections of his motives from his mother, his four sisters and six cousins.

"Mrs. Bates," a nurse he'd never seen before said from the door to the scrub room. "The doctor said you can come back in for a few minutes."

Sarah stood and started away, but she stopped and looked back at him. "Is there any reason my friend can't come in? He loves Grace, too."

"Of course," she answered. "In fact if you have family, maybe you should call—"

"No," Sarah cut in. "There's no one else."

Kip followed, scrubbed and then entered the NICU all the while thinking her parents belonged there praying for the grandchild they'd never even bothered to come see and supporting the daughter they so shamefully ignored.

Grace was in a separate part of the NICU now, isolated from the others. She was back on the ventilator and back on the flat bed. Peter Kelly looked up when they came in. He'd met Pete through Angel Flight fund-raisers but he'd never seen him under circumstances like this.

"Her fever hasn't gone up any more, Sarah," he said, gently. "We have that going for us. We got the cultures back and that's why I called in the lung specialist. He's suggested a new antibiotic. It's the best protocol against the bug she has."

"That's good, right?" Sarah asked, desperate hope in her tone.

Kelly nodded but his expression remained grave. "All antibiotics have risks and this particular one isn't usually used on preemies. In fact, as far as we know, it's never been used on a micro preemie like Grace. It's a risk but I think it's one we have to take. She's not going to fight this off otherwise. You understand what I mean?"

Sarah's lower lip trembled but she sank her teeth into it as if steadying it would steady her. She nodded. Kip put a hand on her shoulder, praying he'd be able to lend her a little strength. "I told you to do whatever you have to do to save her," she said, then asked, "Can I hold her first?"

"Only for a moment. We're trying to keep her cool. It's strange, I know. All along we've been fighting to keep her warm and now—" Pete Kelly shook his head. "The next few hours are pretty critical. If she's going to respond, it'll be soon. And if she has a bad reaction—" He stopped. Took a breath. "Well, that may be sooner."

The look in Pete's eyes was so solemn Kip understood what that meant without a doubt. The antibiotic could kill Grace. Suddenly, being a pilot and having people's lives rely on his skill didn't seem so high pressure an occupation, after all.

Sarah cradled Grace's tiny body in both

hands. Talking softly. Urging her to fight on. Telling her all the plans she had for them when Grace got strong enough to go home. Then Sarah laid her back on the temperature-controlled pad and continued talking to her, petting her head and letting Grace curl her little fingers around her mother's pinky.

Leslie Washington came in behind him and drew Kip's attention. Kip looked at his watch. She didn't work this shift as far as he knew. "I couldn't stay away, either," she explained. "I took night duty for someone. Why don't you pray for our girl. None of us is ready to give up on her. Least of all Grace herself."

"Please, Kip," Sarah said. "She did so good in surgery after you prayed. Hold her. Pray for her. Maybe…"

Sarah had no faith in her own prayers but at least she still believed. Kip bent down and Leslie laid Grace on just one of his hands. Her little bottom rested on the heel of his hand and he was able to support her head and neck with his fingertips. She felt like a feather. Her downy hair was soft against his fingers and she was just about as light. It was hard to believe she was real and alive.

But he could feel her labored breathing.

Her tiny heart beating.

And she was warm. Awfully, awfully warm.

His throat ached with the magnitude of the loss it would be if this tiny human didn't make it. He bit his lip, blinked away the burning tears he just couldn't fight and cleared his throat.

"Lord, You know Grace and what a fighter she is. She needs of Your help right now. And You know Sarah's pain at seeing her child suffer like this because You watched Your Son suffer. This new drug is risky but we know You can make it work safely and well. Let her stay with us. Our lives are but moments to You. Please give Grace her full measure of moments. Make this a time for Grace to thrive. I—" his voice cracked and he had to clear his throat again. "I ask You for the life of this child in the name of Your Son. Amen."

Kip placed Grace back on the temperature-controlled bed, mindful of Pete Kelly's admonition about keeping her cool enough. Then he took a deep breath and turned to Sarah. She nodded, still looking scared but a little more confident. She moved next to the flat bed. "You rest now, baby girl. They're going to give you a new medicine that'll fix you right up. Mommy won't be far away. I'll be back again later. I have faith in you, Grace. You'll be here waiting for me."

Kip followed her out and took the seat next to her on the bench where he'd found her when he arrived.

"I feel as if I'm always thanking you," Sarah said after a few moments. "I told Miriam not to bother you, but I'm glad she did, too. I'm thankful that someone else who loves Grace is here."

"And *I* feel like I'm always apologizing to you. I got your message last night maybe fifteen minutes after you called, but I thought the message was from that afternoon. It seemed like a moot point by then. If I'd known what was going on here…" He shook his head realizing he'd probably said enough. "Well, anyway, I'm sorry I didn't understand your call was urgent."

"It's okay. Really. I don't remember what I even said but I'm sure if I'd mentioned that Grace was sick you'd have called me back when you got in."

He only nodded because what he really wanted to do was correct her. He'd have come running if he'd known Sarah herself needed him but telling her would be a mistake. No matter what Grace's outcome was that night, a stronger bond had already formed between them.

Once again she wrapped her arms around herself and he couldn't watch that lonely gesture again. Nor could he maintain his self-imposed isolation when she was so close and so alone. He reached over and tucked her against his side, resting his cheek against her silky hair as her head came to rest on his shoulder. This was like walking a tightrope and he knew it. One wrong step and someone could get terribly hurt.

Sarah deserved better than another disappointment from someone she cared about. She'd apparently had enough of those to last a lifetime already.

Chapter Twelve

It was hours later that the door to the NICU swung open. Sarah jumped to her feet, her heart pounding in fear. Then within a heartbeat Kip was on his feet right behind her, gripping her shoulders, lending her support and strength. She held her breath as Doctor Kelly stepped into the hall.

He turned around and wore a wide grin. "Her temp's down, Sarah. Her breathing's easier, too. I think we've got this thing licked."

For some reason all she could do was stand there and stare at him. She knew what he'd said and what it meant, but she didn't seem to be able to process it. Maybe she was just afraid to hope.

Her knees started to shake. If Kip hadn't

stepped close behind her and wrapped his arms around her waist, Sarah was sure she'd have folded up in a heap.

"What about the effects of the drug on Grace?" Kip asked, still supporting her both mentally and physically.

"Her labs are looking okay as far as the side effects of the antibiotic. I'd say she's showing no adverse effects of it. Your kid is one feisty little critter, Sarah. Of course, we're going to monitor her closely but she's looking pretty good to me."

"Thanks, Pete. This is great news," Kip said as he moved to her side, keeping his arm wrapped around her waist. "It's great news. Isn't it, Sarah? Sarah? You have to breathe, honey. Take a breath."

Sarah sucked in a great gulp of air. She hadn't even realized she'd been holding her breath. "She's really better?" she asked, still a little breathless.

Doctor Kelly chuckled. "Come on. Let's get you in there to see her. Maybe you'll believe your own eyes."

She looked up at Kip. "You come, too."

"Sure," he said smiling. "Come on. Let's get scrubbing."

Sarah felt giddy and light as air. Kip was as

excited as she was, smiling and scrubbing up with gusto. Sarah breathed a further sigh of relief when they got to Grace's little bed. Her coloring was back to that blessed pink it had picked up after her oxygen flow improved following her surgery. She was cooler to the touch and off the respirator, as well.

Leslie suggested Sarah hold her and see if she was strong enough to take a bottle, one of her newer accomplishments. Once the baby was in her arms, Grace opened her eyes. Kip knelt next to Sarah and chuckled. Grace sought out the sound and looked right at him, and they both could have sworn she smiled around the nipple. They looked at each other then grinned through grateful, happy tears.

Grace took very little of the bottle and was soon sound asleep as if she'd put on all the show for her fan club that she intended to that night. Doctor Kelly was a bit worried about wearing her out so Leslie returned her to her bed.

While they walked toward the elevators, Kip offered her a ride home and Sarah gratefully accepted. Though she was buoyant with relief, exhaustion had crowded in on her now that she knew her child was once again safe and gaining strength.

Sarah was so tired, in fact, she fell asleep practically as soon as Kip steered his pickup onto the highway.

The last thing she remembered was a sign for the Schuylkill Expressway before a lack of motion woke her. She hadn't even opened her eyes when she inhaled the combined scent of old leather and lime. Kip's distinctive scent.

Probably unconsciously seeking his warmth in the chilled pickup, she'd moved over close to him and leaned her head on his shoulder. For just a few moments Sarah absorbed the comfort of having his shoulder to lean on, but then she heard Kip make a small sound that was somewhere between distress and impatience.

"I'm so sorry," she gasped. She sat up and scooted quickly away from him. What had she been thinking? In spite of his affectionate support all night, he'd made his feelings on entanglements very plain.

"It's okay. You were cold and tired."

She nodded and pushed some stray hairs off her face. "I've been up for twenty-four hours and I didn't get much sleep before they called me to tell me Grace was sick. I'd stayed late because she was fussy. I guess she was starting to get sick then."

"It's okay," he repeated. "It gave me some time to think. I know you're tired but would you mind if I came up. There are some things we really need to talk about."

She couldn't imagine what they'd need to talk about unless he wanted to make another, me-lone-bachelor speech. She'd done pretty well managing the last one. She could do it again and send him on his way with a clear conscience. It was the least she could do to pay him back for all his support.

"Sure. I can make hot cocoa. I even have marshmallows," she said trying to sound breezy. That ought to show him she wasn't trying to hook him against his will. Who served a man cocoa as a come-on? Of course she wouldn't know how to be seductive if she tried. And she wouldn't want a man who'd require her to be something other than who she was, anyway.

He nodded, and seemed more sad than irritated so maybe she'd read his intent wrong. She hoped so because she really wasn't in any condition for a confrontation of any kind.

Kip followed her into the garage and up the interior wooden steps. "Have a seat," she said as she passed the stools and the breakfast bar. They could talk with the countertop between them. That ought to make whatever he had to say easier to deal with. But that wasn't to be.

"Sarah. Stop," he said and caught her hand as she hung her purse on the back of one of the dinette chairs. She turned, surprised to see how pained his expression was. And how close he was.

"What's wrong, Kip?"

"This," he said, then his free hand tipped her face up as his lips descended. Of their own accord her eyelids dropped closed. His kiss didn't have the edge it'd had when it morphed into more than a celebration on Grace's behalf. This kiss brought tears to her eyes because it was so bittersweet. After a moment, his hand left her face as his lips left hers. She opened her eyes and wanted to weep at the utter agony written on his kind, handsome features. "Kip, *what* is it?"

"Come on," he said and she realized he still held her hand when he tugged her toward the living room area. "Let's sit in here."

She followed, exhaustion and anxiety chasing away any impatience she'd felt when he'd asked to talk with her. She sat on the sofa and he let go of her hand then sat across from her. He sat for a long moment, his posture identical to the way it had been after he'd arrived at the hospital and sat next to her on the bench—elbows on his thighs, hands clasped and head down. She didn't know if he was praying, thinking or both. What she did know was that, after she'd seen the look in his eyes, she'd give him till dawn if that was how long it took for him to explain what was wrong. A kiss and the emotions it had stirred hardly seemed an answer.

Then he looked up and she was no longer sure about that. "There are things you deserve to know. Things that make my life— my bachelor life—make sense. Things that make not changing it make sense even though I'd give nearly anything to be able to."

"O-kay," she said carefully, more confused than ever.

"My dad died when I was seven," he said.

She nearly interrupted to tell him she knew all the reasons for his bachelor lifestyle from Miriam. But then he went on and she'd be forever thankful she'd decided to count to ten instead cutting in.

"My uncle Galen died two years after my dad. My aunt and six cousins moved in so my

mom and Aunt Emily could pool their resources. Which really meant my mom went
back to work as a nurse and my grandmother
and Aunt Em took care of all of us. I tell them
all—my sisters, cousins and mom—that
living with a baker's dozen of women has me
out of patience with the lot of you." He shot
her a little grin, taking the sting out of his
words. "It's not really a lie because I'm
usually pretty out of patience when they get
on me about not being married. And I can
honestly say I'd never met a woman I thought
I would want to live with even though I've
always wished I could have kids."

"I don't understand what you're saying.
You kissed me and said it was a problem.
Neither of us is attached. I know I pretended
it didn't mean anything when you kissed me
at the hospital but—"

"Uh, Sarah, I didn't believe the act for a
second. You kissed back. You also aren't the
kind of woman to kiss like that with no
feelings involved."

"Oh." She felt a blush heat her face and
looked at the floor. "Then I really don't see
a problem."

"The problem is that no matter what we
feel, it can't go further."

That got her to look back up no matter how embarrassed she was. "Why?"

"For the reason I grew up the way I did. My dad and uncle weren't killed in freak accidents or war or sickness or any number of other random things that shorten lives. They died when their perfectly good hearts just stopped. And my grandfather and great-uncle. And their father. I don't know any further back than that but you get the idea. The weird thing is my nephews will all be fine if history repeats itself. Sons of the Webster women have all been just fine. A few lived into their nineties. But I'm going to die in eight years or less. None of the male line lived more than a few months past their fortieth birthdays. Some not even that long."

She sat in stunned silence, speechless. His days on earth were numbered. Soon she might be grieving another loss. It was too much. She shook her head, and tears welled up in her eyes. "Are you sure they can't help you? What's wrong with your heart?"

"Do you think I haven't tried to find out? They tell me there's nothing wrong. They told my dad and uncle the same thing. My uncle saw his doctor one morning. My cousin came home from school that afternoon and found him sleeping on the sofa— but he wasn't asleep. He was dead."

She gasped.

"You see it, don't you? You know how much it hurt losing your husband after such a short marriage. Imagine how much it would hurt to have years of love just cut off in the blink of an eye. I can't leave someone I love to grieve the way my mom and aunt did. I can't leave *you* that way. Or with the financial and emotional burden of raising my kids alone on top of that. I won't live the rest of my life knowing that if I do the selfish thing and let what we feel blossom and grow, I've condemned you to that. And if we had a son, then I've done this to him. And again to you. My grandmother buried both her sons. My aunt was right to tell me—warn me. It ends with me. No more wives and mothers burying us. *No more.*"

She nodded, biting her lip. She couldn't tell him he was wrong. How could she follow her heart knowing it was destined to be broken in two? Better a crack now than devastation later. If losing Scott had hurt as much as it had, how much worse would it hurt to lose her soul mate?

To lose Kip.

He stood and kissed the top of her head. She looked up, trying to see him through a sheen of tears. "Is there anything I can do for you?"

He smiled sadly. "Be happy. Find some great guy to help raise Amazing Gracie and give her healthy and happy brothers and sisters. Just be happy, love. It's the best any of us can do."

Sarah squeezed her eyes shut and sent the tears that had gathered there cascading down her cheeks. The door shut and she heard him pelting down the steps into the garage. His pickup roared to life, then its sound faded into the distance.

And she was alone.

Again.

Sarah sat in stunned silence for a long time trying to imagine a world without Kip Webster in it somewhere. "Why does life have to be so hard, Lord?" she asked aloud, then when no answer came she dragged herself to bed and turned off her alarm. It was Saturday and nearly dawn so she planned to sleep as long as she could.

But once in bed, she lay staring at the ceiling as it lightened with the rising dawn. Sleep just wouldn't come. Tired as she was, her mind kept running over those devastating moments as Kip poured out his story. She recalled everything she knew about him. She relived every second she'd spent with him. As one thought connected to the other she realized she'd begun comparing him to Scott.

Then she purposely centered her thoughts on her late husband alone. She remembered the fun they'd had. The snowman they'd built the day they'd met when she was so happy to see snow again. And that brought up the misadventure when he'd tried to teach her to ski a month later when she headed down the wrong slope—the double diamond slope—and he'd had to ski alongside her and steer her off to the side. Then there'd been all those lunches in the teachers' lounge when they'd talked about their shared faith and a thousand other subjects that interested them. They just didn't talk about their pasts.

And she remembered his enthusiasm while handling the arrangements for their wedding. He'd made shopping for rings fun too. She chuckled recalling his long, long lists of the things they'd do after they were married. Scuba diving, motor biking, deep-sea fishing, dancing in the moonlight and swimming in it too. Those were the things they'd managed to check off during their Bermuda honeymoon. Those were the only things they'd checked off.

Because then it had been time to say goodbye and he'd stretched that moment by hanging out the window waving until the bus was out of sight. And he was out of her life.

Even though sorting through the memories cemented the truth in her heart that for her he'd been more friend than lover, she had no regrets. She *had* made him happy.

And because of that and Grace, Sarah knew she wouldn't trade a second of their short time together. They would always be good memories and no amount of regret could make them anything but.

Scott hadn't wasted a minute of his life. He'd reached out and squeezed every last moment out of it. She knew he'd died without regret because of that. That had been his final message to her relayed though a medic.

Kip was wrong.

He didn't understand grief. A year—a week—a day together would be better than spending years depriving themselves of happiness and living with the futility of time wasted forever because of the fear of the eventual pain of loss.

He was determined to deny them years' worth of precious moments. Moments that would never happen if he got his way.

He had no right to make a unilateral decision. No right at all.

Sarah slept late the next day. When she got up she called Kip but got his machine. She didn't leave a message but did call Agape Air to see if he was around. Joy told her he'd flown a load of merchandise to Atlanta and wouldn't be back till later in the night. His partner didn't sound any happier about him taking the flight than Sarah was.

She revised her plan. Sunday. She'd see him Sunday at the Christmas Eve service and talk some sense into him. But Kip was a no-show there, too.

Monday was Christmas. She went to CHOP to spend the morning with Grace. She'd ordered some of the little T-shirts off the Internet site that Kip had found in the magazine. His thoughtfulness still touched her. There she learned that Kip had delivered a gift to the NICU for Grace. It was a baby doll the exact size, coloring and look of a micro preemie like Grace.

One of the nurses told her she'd seen the dolls on the Internet too, linked to the site where she'd bought the cute little tees. They were specially made by a company that produced handmade, hand-painted baby dolls their customers could have built and painted to look exactly the way they wanted. The little blond baby doll with the soft downy hair must have cost him a small fortune.

Sarah took it home with her and laid it in Grace's crib to hold the place for her daughter till she could come home. Then she headed across the drive to Miriam's where she'd been invited to spend the day.

Sarah couldn't wait to see Kip now for yet another reason. She missed him and wanted to thank him for his thoughtfulness. And the longer she waited to try showing him the error of this thinking, the more nervous she got that he wouldn't listen.

She arrived only to learn that at the last minute, Kip had changed his plans. Instead of spending the day with his sister and the rest of the family, he'd decided to fly to Florida to spend the holidays with his mother and her husband. He wasn't to return till after New Year's Day.

Miriam thought the idea of having all his sisters and nieces and nephews under one roof had scared him away. Sarah knew better.

She had.

After an early dinner, Sarah returned to the NICU to spend the evening with Grace. Her friend Mary Jane arrived late on Tuesday the twenty-sixth with Sarah's car. For the rest of the week, they divided their time between visits with Grace and seeing historic sights in and around Philadelphia. There were more to see than Sarah had imagined so the week was thankfully a busy one without much time for thought.

Grace was once again swiftly gaining ground. Seeing her baby actually beginning to interact with her environment and caregivers gave Sarah great hope that Grace had a healthy, happy future ahead. For the first time there was talk of Grace going home. The entire NICU team were shooting for some time in early spring. Sarah celebrated the news with Mary Jane but couldn't help wishing she were celebrating with Kip.

Mary Jane flew home to West Virginia on Saturday the thirtieth and Sarah watched

Miriam and Gary's brood on New Year's Eve to give the couple a night on the town. Sarah tried to put Kip out of her mind as much as she could but it wasn't easy because everywhere she looked in her apartment she could picture him from the day he helped move her things in. It was no different at the hospital or church.

School started up again on January second. It might be a new year but Sarah had been forced to carry old baggage into it. Blessedly, her nerves had disappeared and she was fighting mad again.

She checked the bulletin board as soon as she arrived at school that morning and learned much to her delight that there was basketball practice scheduled for three that afternoon. Just this once, Grace would have to forgive her for being late for their time together. Because Sarah had every intention of ambushing Kip after practice.

What was the old adage? All's fair in love and war. Well, there was plenty of love and this was war. She intended to tell him he had no right to make the decision he had on his own. That it should be her choice, too.

Her parents had made decisions that had

affected her for years and deprived her of their guidance and love.

Sarah Harris Bates was done suffering in silence, which Kip Webster would find out as soon as she ran him to ground!

Chapter Thirteen

Kip watched the varsity basketball team horsing around as they headed for the showers. They'd done great in their first practice since before the holidays. One of the senior stars tossed a final ball toward the basket and turned away before it threaded neatly through the net, supremely confident of his aim.

This crew was a real handful. But they were good kids and he was glad the seniors would get their chance in front of the college scouts. He smiled and returned the wave of the last player to exit the gym into the locker room.

After racking the basketballs, Kip pivoted away and loped across the gym to grab his jacket out of the small coach's office where he'd left it. He had a week-long charter scheduled in a little over two hours. Once he was sure the team had cleared out, he had to be on his way.

He nearly jumped out of his skin when he strode into the closet-sized office and heard Sarah say, "How was your Christmas?"

He stopped just inside the door and drank in the sight of her. She'd scarcely been out of his thoughts since the last time he saw her. No matter how hard he tried he couldn't erase the sight of her crying over his destiny and the relationship they would never have. But no matter how much that sight haunted him and no matter how much he'd missed her, he had to save her from the grief his aunt, mother and grandmother had suffered. His own pain would be worth it if she eventually found happiness.

He tried to sound impersonal and detached when he answered her question. "My Christmas was fine. You shouldn't be here, Sarah. I don't want to have to give up this church or my coaching role with the team but I will if it'll keep us apart. I thought you agreed with me."

She nodded. "I did at first. But then I realized that it was cowardly of me. I never saw myself in that light before, and I have to admit I didn't like it. What about you? Are you going to throw away what you admit we could build between us out of fear? I never thought of you as a coward either."

Kip swallowed. He didn't know how much more he could take. He walked around behind the desk and sank carefully into the chair. "I'm only afraid of hurting you. I'll be in the throne room, basking in the glory of the Lord's presence. You'll be back here dealing with grief and money problems."

"Let's look at finances, shall we? Is your partnership in Agape Air written up in a way that says the partner who predeceases the other gives back the proceeds to the surviving member? Or have you named heirs who will benefit?"

He stared at her. The woman was smart. He'd give her that. She was also dangerous to his peace of mind. "Thirty percent of the Agape's profits will go into an educational trust for my nieces and nephews. Twenty percent reverts to Joy since she'll be the one running the company."

He'd purposely said *will* and not *would* because he wanted her to understand there was no chance of anything else happening.

A little frown crinkled up her forehead. "My, you do think ahead. You have real control issues, you know."

The sarcasm from Sarah took him by surprise. He hadn't been ready for that. "These events aren't that far ahead at all, Sarah."

She shrugged. "My point is that any children we have will be cared for."

He gritted his teeth at her use of the certainties he'd lived with for fourteen years and had tried to use in order to bring home to her the reality of his life—and death. She had her ducks in a row. He'd give her that, too.

Before he could think of any further rebuttal, she went on. "So then there is the grief you mentioned. You think it won't be a comfort to me that I'll know you're happy? And that I'll know I'll see you again? You'd be very wrong. Been there. Done that. Bought the T-shirt. It is a comfort to know Scott is in a better place even though he's not here with Grace and me. But, you're right. There *is* grief. There *will* be grief for the loss of you."

"I'm trying to save you that," he told her emphatically.

She shook her head. "Let me tell you something about grief. It's lessened, *not* heightened, when you can look back on wonderful memories. Not for one second have I ever wished I hadn't met Scott. Not for one second have I ever wished I hadn't let him talk me into marrying him. He gave me Grace. Even if he hadn't given me her, he gave me funny, lighthearted, spontaneous memories. I wouldn't trade them for an absence of the grief I felt at his passing.

"Would you wish away your seven years' worth of memories of your father? Do you think your grandmother would wish away the memories of her sons? Do you think your mother wishes she'd never met your father? Ask her, Kip. Ask her if she would have refused to share his life when he asked if he'd also told her about his family history. *Ask* her."

She stood, apparently having said her piece. He should have been relieved. But once she left, he knew he'd be bereft of her presence. He'd no longer be able to watch the sun dancing in her silky hair. He wouldn't have that pert nose to admire. When she left she'd take those beautifully shaped lips with her—the lips he yearned to kiss into silence.

"I have one more question, then I have to get to the hospital," she added. "What makes you think I won't walk in front of a car next year?"

Kip nearly smiled. Serious and heart-wrenching as this conversation was, it struck him that he'd found one more appealing and endearing quality about Sarah. He enjoyed matching wits with her as much as he enjoyed laughing with her. Then he thought of a way to combat the clever way she'd twisted his logic with a twist of his own. "All the more reason I'm not the man for you. If you're that careless, our children will be completely orphaned in eight years. Who will raise them?"

Sarah stared at him gravely for a long moment. She was good at creating those still moments during which she thought about her answer without looking uncomfortable for not having a ready answer. She crossed her arms and those soft-as-velvet eyes pierced his heart. "I would imagine your sisters would step in, but think about this, Kip. If we aren't married and something does happen to me, what would Grace's life be like? How long do you think it will be before my parents stick her in a nice, tidy little boarding school where she'll have to look to strangers for guidance and affection?"

With that last zinger delivered, she wheeled away and walked back out of his life.

* * *

The motel near the airport in Hollywood, Maryland was a combination of suites and short stay rooms. And not bad as far as comforts went for a tiny town an hour south-east of Washington, Kip decided as he perused the services brochure. He might just head on down to the health club and work off a little of his frustration.

His clients on this week-long trip were a group of four businessmen who were trying to sell the various branches of the armed forces some sort of computer training system. In typical government inefficiency the people responsible for those decisions weren't all located at the Pentagon where he would have expected but were stationed at various bases around the county. The salesmen had too much expensive equipment to risk on clumsy airport baggage handlers, so they'd hired Agape.

Tomorrow they'd be off to San Diego, and after a one-day layover, they'd head to the San Francisco Bay Area for two days. Then it was on to Colorado Springs before returning them home. He'd be gone a full week by then.

Kip had managed to keep his mind

focused on his flying but now, in the near silence of his motel room, it strayed back to the confrontation with Sarah earlier in the day. He couldn't help wondering if she was right. Or if her analysis was wishful thinking? Then again maybe he'd been wrong all this time? Could he even ask his mother the question Sarah had challenged him to ask, knowing it might open a potentially hot topic?

He sighed. Sarah was right about his memories of his dad. He wouldn't trade them. But would his mother?

There was really no way to find out but to ask.

Before he could chicken out, Kip picked up his cell phone and called his mom. He nearly hung up when it started to ring, but then she answered.

"Mom, it's Kip," he said when he heard her sunny voice.

"Hi, honey. How's the pilot biz?"

"Fine, Mom. How's Sam? Did he enjoy the golf tourney?"

"He loved it and did well. We're so glad we bought a place on the edge of the course. He gets in so much more practice these days. Which leaves me more time for my hobbies."

"Are you happy, Mom?" he asked, his tone serious.

"Happy? Son, you were just here. Couldn't you tell?"

Kip relaxed against the pile of pillows on the bed and crossed his ankles. "I just wondered if you're afraid all the time that something might happen to him. You know, the way it did with Dad."

His mother chuckled. "Ever hear the old saying: The only sure things in this world are death and taxes. In case you're wondering, it's true. Much as I love Sam, I know he'll die one day and that I may be the one left behind. I refuse to live in fear, especially since it could just as easily go the other way. Me first. He'd be the one grieving a second wife's death, then."

Kip struggled to voice the question Sarah had challenged him to ask. Finally he just blurted it out. "Mom, are you ever sorry about marrying Dad?"

"Kip! Of course not. I loved your father to distraction! Why would you think I'd be sorry?"

"Well, because he left you in such a financial mess with five kids to raise on your own. And you cried at night for months."

"I loved him. I missed him terribly. But by wishing away my marriage I'd have wished away my children. And you know the financial mess wasn't that bad. We had a house paid for with his insurance money. But five kids are a lot of expense. I loved all of you too much to ever wish for the easy way out."

"Even the one just like him," he added, waiting to see if she understood.

"Do you mean you because you're a man or because you look so very much like your father? Why would you think I'd regret having a son who reminds me of Kevin?"

Full of nervous energy, Kip got to his feet and paced across the room to the windows. "Maybe because I'll die the way he did," he said and even he heard the tension in his voice.

His mother's shock was evident in her one-word reply. "What?"

"I know, Mom. I know about his heart. And Uncle Galen's. I know about my grandfather and my great-grandfather. I remember Grandmom at his funeral and at Uncle Galen's and how she cried." He raked a hand through his hair. "I know it all. I know that you'll live to see me dead. I've known for years. Since I was eighteen."

"Emily." His mother's voice was exasperated, then angry. "She just had to meddle!"

"I'm glad she did. I've always worried about leaving some poor woman grieving and burdened with my kids."

"Stop right there, mister! How dare you?"

Her anger shocked Kip. His mother hadn't shouted at him like that since he put the snake in his sister's bed. "Mom—"

"Don't you *Mom* me. You children were your father's *and* mine and you were never a burden. And I know Emily put that in your head. I heard her saying it enough."

"But you had to work so hard."

"No harder than I did as a housewife. And not harder than Emily, who I mean to have a serious talk with."

"Mom, I didn't call to cause trouble between you two. I only asked because Sarah said—"

His mother sounded way too interested when she said, "Sarah? Your sister's new tenant?"

Thinking on his feet Kip replied, "We got into a philosophical discussion about my situation," he said, trying to sound nonchalant and keeping strictly to the truth. It had been a discussion on his philosophy on his life. And his death.

"What situation?" she asked, then before he could answer his mother audibly sucked in a shocked breath. "Oh, honey, please tell me this isn't why you're single. No. Don't say a thing. You already more or less admitted it. This is why you've barely ever dated. Kip, you're wasting your life."

"I have a very full life, Mom," he told her, trying to soothe her worry. But since meeting Sarah he felt as if the blinders had been ripped from his eyes. Occasional dissatisfaction and lonesomeness had turned into discontent and loneliness.

"Kip, you're busy but that isn't the rich full life you deserve. Oh, I just want to slap that meddlesome old woman upside the head!"

"Don't kid me," said Kip, trying to lighten her anger. "You don't have a violent bone in your body. And may I remind you she's three years younger than you are, Mom, so you really ought to watch calling her old," he added, hoping to distract his mother.

"Oh, Emily was old the day she was born. And she's as needy today as she was then, too," his mother said, scorn rife in the tone. "Why do you think she moved in with us? Because she couldn't survive on her own, let alone with those girls, that's why. I couldn't sit by and watch that happen.

"Now about this Sarah I'm hearing so many praises about, tell me all about her and don't leave out a thing."

How to describe Sarah? Should he tell her about her sweet disposition. Considering their last conversation and the way she'd gone to bat for her child, maybe sweet wasn't the right word. But most of the time sweet was close.

He thought about telling his mom about her crushing guilt for being angry at her parents when she had a right to be angry at them. And the way she tried to figure out what God was thinking and, yes, the way she tried to reason away her anger at Him. But that had been something she'd shared with him in confidence so he didn't feel he was free to talk about that.

Maybe he should describe her chestnut hair. Or her big brown velvety eyes framed by those long lush eyelashes or the perfect arch of the eyebrows over them. Her sweet smile was certainly memorable. He himself smiled thinking about the way she always bit that full bottom lip when she was worried or upset.

He'd finally decided to go with just the

facts of how he'd met her when his mother spoke. "Did you ever hear that sometimes silence can be eloquent?" she asked, her voice soft with love for him. "Don't give up on life, Kip. And don't give up on Sarah. Go home to her and tell her how you feel. Then marry the girl so I can start buying pretty dresses for my new granddaughter. I love you, son. Please don't waste the life God gave you by trying to control future events. That's the Lord's job."

Kip realized he wanted nothing more but how could he condemn Sarah to more grief? He said good-night and hung up, wondering which of them was right—he and his aunt Emily or his mom and Sarah?

Chapter Fourteen

"I'm sorry, Sarah. I thought you knew," Miriam said with pity in her eyes as they sat across from each other in the teachers' lounge during lunch on Wednesday. "He won't be back till late in the afternoon on the ninth."

No, she hadn't known. But then why would she? It wasn't as if they'd talked. She'd confronted. He'd defended. Their last meeting had been more like of a fencing match on a piste. Tierce. Parry. Riposte. A jaunty touché and she'd walked out. She'd played it wrong. Now she didn't know if she'd drawn a black card and been disqualified or if she'd made her point.

Confused. Hurt. Disheartened, Sarah tried to cover her roiling emotions. "He has a right to leave town. The man is working. And he certainly doesn't have to check with me. He owes me nothing. I'm the one who owes him."

"Still, I think he should have told you. I don't care what you say, Kip cares very deeply for both you and Grace."

Sarah nodded. She knew that. His feelings or lack of them weren't the problem. But there was no way she would reveal Kip's inner torture to Miriam. Kip's sister meant well but Sarah had learned that expecting discretion from her would be like expecting to slice a turkey with a chain saw. Her fellow teacher and landlord didn't seem to have a subtle bone in her body.

Sarah looked down at her lunch bag, stood and left the teachers' lounge. She was no longer interested in the egg salad sandwich she'd packed for lunch. It didn't matter what Miriam said. Kip's actions spoke louder and louder all the time. He refused to reconsider.

Hurrying to her classroom, hoping to get there, close the door and have a good cry or a good scream, she rounded the corner and ran smack into Pastor Dillon.

Jim looked on the edge of panic when he

zeroed in on her tear-filled eyes. Then he took a deep breath. "Is it Grace?"

She shook her head and a tear rolled free.

"Then come to my office. Maybe a long talk will help. I promise if you cry, I won't run. Holly would kill me! But worse, I'd disappoint my boss again."

His self-deprecating smile put her at ease and she nodded. Maybe he *could* help. Sarah followed him into his modest office. She noticed he once again closed his hall door, but opened the inner door to the outer office where the church secretary worked. She heard him tell her he was in conference with one of the female teachers, then he stepped back in and moved toward his desk, leaving the door open.

Sarah stared at the open door. She really didn't want her conversation overheard. She worked there and was building a base of at least acquaintances among her co-workers. Uncomfortable, she asked, "Do we have to have the door open, Pastor?"

He nodded. "I never speak to a female alone with a door not open. It's just a rule I was taught by a friend early in my ministry. It avoids even the chance of creating gossip and a possible scandal. Relax, Sarah. Nancy knows to switch over to transcribing a book I'm writing. She puts on earphones and can't hear a thing we say. Now, suppose you tell me why you looked like you were about to erupt out there?"

"Because I'm furious, Pastor."

His forehead knitted for a moment. "You've had a lot go wrong in your life this last year. I'm sure it gets overwhelming at times. And make it Jim."

She nodded. "Jim." Sarah took a deep breath. "I feel guilty over my anger. And I feel like the guilt could crush me some days. I can't pray anymore. I don't think He listens."

"God the Father doesn't want us to feel fruitless guilt over our sins. He wants our repentance. Then He wants us to forget our transgressions and move on. We're washed clean in His eyes by His Son's shed blood and the sacrifice Jesus made on the Cross. Your sins are invisible to God once you repent of them."

Sarah sighed. "But it's pretty hard to repent when you're still angry and getting angrier every day," she said. "I was very angry at God for Scott's death and Grace's early delivery but I think Kip may have helped me work that out. I think God wanted me here and those circumstances got me here. I may have even made a mistake in marrying Scott. You see, I had doubts but I let him talk me into the marriage. Still, I can see where the Lord may have used my mistake for the good," she explained.

She of course had no intention of revealing her feelings for Kip since he and Jim Dillon were such close friends. She couldn't do that to Kip or Jim. It wouldn't be fair.

Also now that she'd started talking to Jim, something vitally important had occurred to her. Because she'd been so alone during the terribly frightening circumstances of Grace's life, she had come to rely more heavily on Kip than she ever had on anyone. Therefore she'd gotten to know him quickly and well. She'd gotten close enough to the heart of the man to fall in love with him in a way she never had with Scott.

She and Kip had bonded over Grace's problems.

"Don't get me wrong, I cared about Scott but I know he's happy in heaven," she told Jim. "But there's something underlying it all." She went on to explain about her parents and how they'd always pushed her to the background of their lives. "They've seeded count-less schools, churches and small hospitals all over Africa and South America with their own money and funds from sponsoring churches."

"Their own money?"

She nodded. "My parents both came from very wealthy families. They're what's often called trust-fund babies. Considering what some of their counterparts did with their lives, they look like saints. I guess in many ways they are. They were both only children raised in privileged environments. It was the early seventies when they met in college and started dating seriously. They were both saved at a crusade in the Los Angeles area.

"They got married and walked away from their world of wealth and privilege not long after that. There's a lot about them to admire. But I think my impending birth must have been a bit of a shock. I was born in Kenya in nineteen eighty. They had thousands of children already and I've always felt they didn't need me." She nearly groaned. "Oh, I sound so pathetic!"

Jim leaned back in his chair and crossed his arms. "What you sound is lonely. You feel cheated. You feel abandoned and you have a right to. Yes, their work is admirable as is what they've done with their lives but their treatment of their daughter from where I'm sitting didn't measure up to what the Lord expects of parents."

She nodded but felt unworthy of his understanding. She once again tried to explain away their desertion. "The world they live in can be a dangerous place, though. After a close call when I was seven, they put me in a top-notch Christian boarding school in the mountains north of San Francisco. I really believe their intention was to keep me safe. They moved on from there and took me with them again. But then tensions rose in that country too, and they sent me to another school, this time in Switzerland. Life pretty much repeated like that. I've been in schools in Australia, France, South Africa, back to San Francisco. Till high school when they seemed to forget me altogether. I was lonely and I needed them. I learned not to say that or they'd tell me all about how much good they were doing. How my new school would open up more possibilities for me. That I needed to live the adventure. Their message seemed to be that I was being petty because their other children were so needy and I was so lucky. I never got their emotional support. I still need it and I still don't get it."

Jim pursed his lips deep in thought, then he sat forward. "Suppose we try to think about them as imperfect people. They were faced with a dilemma and they chose the course they did. I wouldn't have. You wouldn't have. But they did. Try to think of it this way. You make decisions concerning Grace hoping they'll be for her good. I don't imagine your parents made their decisions hoping you'd wind up feeling the way you do. They had to think they were doing the right thing."

The pastor shook his head and looked heavy-hearted. "The number of misguided members of His flock is depressing. Just because your parents are serving God they were never exempt from being good parents. In ignoring you and your early complaints, they've offended the very God they try so hard to serve. I don't know them, but it sounds very much like they turned their backs on the world of money and privilege to avoid having it become an idol to them."

Sarah was amazed. Kip and Miriam had been so right about how insightful Jim was. "That's exactly what they told me."

Jim smiled sadly. "As I said, I see that their intentions were good, but I also think it's possible that they traded one form of idolatry for another."

"Idolatry? I don't understand. They're good Christians. Idolatry sounds a bit harsh."

"I know," Jim Dillon said with a nod. "At first glance it does sound over the top and it sounds nearly impossible in the modern world, but consider this." He stopped and thought for a long moment. "Anything we put between us and the Lord, and between us and His will for us, is idolatry. We don't have to fashion a golden calf and physically bow down to it to make something an idol. For me it was booze. For someone else it can be pride. Or a love of cars or a business or just making a lot of money. For your parents it may well have been their record of establishing all those missions you mentioned. Or their work among the poor."

"I don't understand. Jesus told the rich young man that if he wanted everlasting life he should sell all he had, give it to the poor and follow him. But the young man went away sad because he had so much and couldn't sell it. My parents did all that."

"What Jesus was saying was that those things the young man couldn't stand to sell were too important to him. He put them above God. Your parents may have just made what they thought were good decisions with regard to you but something blinded them to your needs. Somehow they ignored the child God gave them to raise and nurture. In doing that they ignored His will for them."

She nodded and as understanding began to dawn she began to feel sorry for her parents. Maybe they'd been misguided and not her.

"A lot of us have to come to a realization of what our idol is," he went on. "Most people have at least one we battle with. Is yours anger? Righteous though it started out to be? Has that childhood anger translated into your adult anger at God over the other things that have gone wrong in your life? They were also beyond your control as were the decisions your parents made for you." He shrugged. "Only you can answer that question. Only they can answer theirs."

"Then what do I do with all this anger?" she asked, recognizing at last what it was doing to her.

"Whatever your answer is, whatever theirs is, Sarah, you have to let go of your portion of this. You need to pray for them. You have to forgive them before your anger moves to hate. Anger and hate are both destructive emotions. They drag us down and only serve to separate us from God and His will for us. Forgive them and then move on with your life so *you* can be the good parent to Grace that the Father would have you be."

Sarah nodded. "I can try."

"What may help is for you to remember that ultimately *God* is your Father. Not the man who you feel forgot his duty to you. Embrace that thought. Your Father in heaven wants all good for you the way a father should. He sent good people into your life all along when your parents' decisions kept them out of it."

Sarah nodded. Yes, He had. Her many teachers. The parents of friends. Especially Scott. He'd made her feel lighthearted for the first time. And Kip had given her security even if he couldn't afford to give it to her forever. She stood and glanced at her watch. She had fifteen minutes before classes resumed.

Jim stood then, too. "Suppose you go into the sanctuary and spend a few minutes with your Father." He rubbed his hands together and grinned. "I'll go up to the art room. The kids can draw me for awhile."

"Thanks," she told him and a stray thought

made her grin. "I have first, sixth and freshman coming in this period. Try not to be too insulted at how their likenesses of you turn out."

He chuckled. "You forget, Jonah is my son."

As an artist, Jonah made a great mathematician. Chuckling, Sarah left the office and made her way into the sanctuary. It was an awe-inspiring space. She'd learned it had originally been nothing but the skeleton of a barn when Jim's young church pooled their resources and bought it. The Tabernacle had grown out of a bible study that met in a fire hall. They'd refurbished the barn with only the help of those original church members, many of whom Jim met on construction jobs—his previous occupation.

She looked up at the beautiful rugged beams then let her eyes trail downward to the cross at the back of the low stage. It was suspended from those rugged beams by three artfully rusted lengths of chain. According to church lore the cross had been fashioned by Jim from a couple of leftover beams and hung where it still was, and the church was then literally built around it.

She sat midway down the middle aisle, and stared at that old rugged cross with the refrain from the hymn running through her head. The words were so appropriate it brought more tears to her eyes.

So I'll cherish the old rugged cross,
Till my trophies at last I lay down;
I will cling to the old rugged cross,
And exchange it some day for a crown.

"I'm so sorry, Lord God," she whispered. "I'm sorry for my anger at You and that I manufactured it from my anger at Mother and Father. I see it now. *You* aren't them. *They* aren't You. They're just flawed representatives of You. They really do nearly worship their work, don't they? Their missions are their trophies. Please send someone to show them the way back to You and You alone."

A smile just seemed to bloom on her face and in her heart. "I don't think I need them anymore. Your love is enough. And Lord, could you please, please wake Kip up to all he's missing in life. Even if I'm not the person You've chosen for him, don't let him waste the rest of his life. I hope I haven't read You wrong and that you do want Kip and me for each other. But Your will be done, Lord. If I was only sent here to show him what he's missing and to help him deal with his problem and then walk away—so be it. I just want what's best for him."

Sarah just sat there for a few minutes, humming the refrain again and absorbing the peace she'd been missing for so so long.

The rest of Sarah's week was much less trying than the beginning. Her reconciliation with God made the continued silence from Kip a little easier to bear as did Grace's continued improvement. But as the week ended and a new one began, she still hadn't heard from him and she began to lose hope that she'd managed to change his mind.

Sarah prayed constantly for him anyway. She'd meant her prayer after talking with Jim. She wanted Kip happy more than she wanted him in her life. She'd already come to the decision that if he did refuse to act on his feelings for her, then she was going to have to make some more changes in her life. The longer the silence went on, the more it looked as if she'd be moving and looking for another job.

She couldn't continue to rent an apartment over his sister's garage because seeing each other would be too painful, and he could hardly be expected to give up visiting his sister's home. She also refused to let Kip be the one to leave The Tabernacle. It had been his church first and he was more than just a member. He was an icon around there. It seemed only right for her to be the one to bow out.

She left for CHOP at the end of the school day on Tuesday as usual, her heart aching now that a week of silence had gone by since she'd last seen him. Her mind was so focused on her thoughts that she didn't even notice the middle-aged couple sitting outside the NICU. She just breezed past them on her way to the scrub room.

"Sarah?" a tentative female voice called softly.

She froze then turned back to the bench where she and Kip had spent those awful hours the night Grace had nearly died. The night she'd have done nearly anything to hear that voice. Adam and Theresa Harris both stood and took a few steps forward.

Anger surged through Sarah before she even fully comprehended that they were really there but she beat it down. She'd forgiven them. But that didn't mean she wasn't shocked to see them. "What are you doing here?" she asked.

They both stopped several feet from her. "We came to apologize, Sarah. And to meet our granddaughter," her father said.

She stared. They'd come to apologize. For which of a thousand offenses? She had her anger pretty much under control. They weren't bad people. Just misguided and neglectful.

She took a moment to just look at them, a little bewildered by their presence. She had wanted this moment for so long but now that it was here she realized she didn't even know them anymore.

She guessed they looked like any other middle-aged couple still living partially in the seventies. The hippie influence was still there in her mother's long pinned-up hair, tie-dyed T-shirt and ruffled prairie skirt. Her father's dark hair was a little grayer. He'd adopted the camp shirt safari style over the years. Neither of them had ever cared about appearances or their own creature comforts.

She really had forgiven them, she realized, but her forgiveness didn't make them right or negate the need of an apology either.

"Apologize for what?" she asked. It struck her then what an odd family they were, standing ten feet apart when they hadn't seen each other in over three years.

Her father, never particularly gregarious, looked at the floor. A blush had colored his cheeks when he looked back up. "All of it. Your young man wrote us. I had a nanny who called it tearing a strip off of someone. We never realized, Sarah. Truly."

"My young man?" She'd heard of military letters going awry. She'd gotten one from Scott the day after his funeral. And, of course, she'd known he was furious about their suggestion that he donate the money to their mission that he'd offered for their airfare. Money she'd tried to tell him they didn't need. But Scott didn't tend to listen to anyone who got in the way of what he wanted. He wheedled. He cajoled. He charmed. She saw that now too. "Scott wrote you before he died?"

"No. The letter was from Kip Webster. He said he was the Angel Flight pilot who flew you and Grace here to Philadelphia. He said you'd become friends, though he seemed to care more than just as a friend."

Sarah felt a surge of love for Kip. He always went the extra mile. And once again he'd shown how much he cared. Not by word but by deed.

"Scott was angry about the wedding and I confess we didn't understand his real objection," her father went on. "He seemed more angry over not getting us to cooperate and with the money issue. We were in a very precarious position at the time. If we'd left, we wouldn't have gotten back in to the country. So…" he trailed off and shook his head. "That no longer matters except that we realize we should have been there. At your wedding. At his funeral. After Grace was born. Webster laid it out so that even we saw his point, emotionally blind though we seem to be."

"I'm afraid neither of us thought about what it was we should have been doing where your feelings and emotions were concerned," her mother added, taking another step forward. "We've been so wrapped up in the doing of the Lord's work that we forgot about the lesson of Mary and Martha. We didn't sit and listen to Him but busied ourselves with what we thought He wanted of us."

"And Kip wrote you?"

"To set us straight," her mother said.

"He did a good job," her father added, grimacing. "We feel just awful that in all the striving to help others we somehow forgot the person He gave us to care for. I know it isn't an excuse but our parents handed us off to others, too. Sending you off to boarding schools when having you with us wasn't practical or safe…well…it seemed perfectly acceptable. We counted ourselves as being wonderful parents because we kept you with us for seven years and brought you along after that whenever it seemed safer. We patted ourselves on the backs because the schools we sent you to were based on biblical principles."

Her mother wiped away a tear. "Except as Kip Webster pointed out, all the adventurous school-hopping didn't broaden your horizons but kept you from having a stable environment. And he mentioned the holidays when the other children went home. You had no home to go to except the homes of teachers or other students whose parents agreed to give you a holiday. We're so so very sorry, Sarah. We never meant for you to feel lonely and abandoned. We're hoping we can find a way to make it all up to you."

Sarah clutched her coat in front of her. "I'm not sure you can, Mother," she said truthfully, though her mother's tears touched her. "I forgive you. I forgave you after a long talk with my new pastor. He made me see that my anger at you had spilled over into my relationship with God. But I'm nearly thirty.

It's a little late. I'd like to try too but I'm not exactly sure where to begin."

Theresa looked at Adam Harris, troubled.

"Suppose we just take it one step at a time," her father said. "May we meet our granddaughter?"

Sarah nodded. She supposed Grace was as good a place to start as any. But her main concern now was her daughter. Her parents were forgiven for slighting Sarah herself but if they hurt Grace, that would be the end of any reconciliation. It would have nothing to do with anger or hatred but her own resolve to care for the child God had given her. Grace was her number one priority when she came to Philadelphia and she would be Sarah's main concern from now on.

Chapter Fifteen

Sarah spoke to one of Grace's nurses so that her parents could enter the NICU. Because they had come in directly from their flight from Africa they were asked to shower and were given a full set of scrubs to wear instead of just a sterile gown to go over their street clothes. The nurse taught Theresa and Adam how to scrub while Sarah went in and began to feed Grace.

"Oh, goodness, she's so small," her mother gasped when she came into the NICU just as Grace finished her miniature bottle. "And she's so thin."

Sarah gave a mental sigh. Her mother's reaction didn't have Kip's nonchalance toward Grace's appearance but she'd seen worse responses. "She's more than doubled her weight, Mother," Sarah replied, knowing she sounded defensive. To Sarah, Grace was the most beautiful child God had ever created.

Sarah smiled at a sudden revelation. She was blessed in an unusual way by Grace and her early birth. There was something very special and exciting about watching her baby develop in ways that most mothers never got to see. They had to wonder what was going on inside them, or try to decipher a grainy ultrasound. But Sarah got to see it all. Up close and tangible.

So while Grace had been more of a worry than the average child, she blessed Sarah with more memories and achievements to enjoy than the average baby would, as well. It didn't completely counteract all the worry but it was a reward of sorts.

Sarah looked at her mother. She'd heard real fear in her voice when she'd spoken. *At least she really seems to care,* Sarah thought as her mother spoke again. "It's just that I had pictured her looking like a newly delivered healthy baby—just smaller. If she's doubled her weight why is she still so thin?"

"She doesn't have the fat layer of a full-term baby," Sarah explained. "They grow to their birth length, then they put on weight to round them out toward the end of the gestation period. Grace didn't get the chance to do any of that. She's remarkable not just because her birth weight was so low. Her gestation period was extremely short, too."

Her father must have entered when neither of them noticed. He rested his hand on his wife's shoulder. "She doesn't look much different than many of the babies in famine regions, dear, and warmth isn't usually a problem in our part of the world."

"Is that why she wears the little hat?" her mother asked.

Sarah nodded. "Keeping her warm enough isn't as hard as it was to keep her cool. Did Kip write you before or after Grace got sick?"

"After Grace was sick," her father replied. "He got our mailing address from Dr. Prentice, so it got to us relatively quickly. In his letter he said you'd had no one to wait with you during Grace's surgery or her illness but him." There was regret in her father's eyes and guilt. "How ill was she when she got sick? He only said it had been dangerous."

Sarah once again fought back an angry

response when she remembered those dark hours as Grace grew weaker and Sarah's hope had begun to wane. But she couldn't react in anger. How could she expect God to forgive her sins if she didn't do the same for her parents? Jim hadn't said it would be easy and it wasn't. It was harder to forgive their neglect of Grace than it was the years they had neglected Sarah herself. Another sudden revelation came to Sarah. It was harder to forgive sins against your child than those committed against yourself. But she had to do it.

"She was very sick. She had pneumonia. We'd all about given up hope. It was the first time I felt really hopeless." She went on to explain the drug and the chance she'd been forced to take by giving permission to use it.

"And there were no ill effects?" Adam asked.

Sarah shook her head. "It was a big risk but the Lord must have something He wants her to do here on earth. She's doing fine now and all the tests on her liver and kidneys were good, too."

"When Grace was ill, Kip Webster men-·tioned he'd been a while finding out. How long were you alone?" her mother asked. The guilt in her voice reminded Sarah of the guilt she'd carried and about Jim's admonishment that once we confess our sin to God, guilt has no place in our lives.

"About fifteen or so hours but when Kip found out, he came right away."

Tears once again entered her mother's eyes as she pulled a chair up next to Sarah. "I'm so sorry we weren't here. I feel so guilty just looking at her and seeing what you've had to deal with on top of losing her father."

"We both do," her father said. "And there's guilt beyond the subject of our neglect of you and Grace. If I could turn back the clock, you'd be seven years old again and we'd leave Africa with you. Just driving here we saw that we could have found plenty of the Lord's work to do in places that would have been safer for you. Sarah, your mother wasn't sure sending you away to boarding schools was right until I convinced her you'd be better off."

"I had a mouth, Adam," her mother protested. "I let myself be talked into it because I knew she'd be in a Christian academy and because, frankly, I still wasn't sure I was cut out to be a mother. In hindsight I think it's a miracle you have any faith left at all in the

God your father and I supposedly have been serving, Sarah."

Sarah nodded and rubbed Grace's back. "I have to admit I very nearly turned my back on God after Grace was born," she told them truthfully, "but He put Grace and me in the right places and then He put the right people in our lives to stop that from happening. First Kip; then the pastor who's also my boss, were able to help me put the past into perspective."

Seeing a look of further distress pass between her parents, Sarah went on, "Look, I don't want you to feel guilty about the past. Once I would have reveled in knowing you were wracked with guilt but I'd have been wrong. I forgave you. I forgive you now. And I hope I'll keep forgiving you every time I'm reminded of a memory that hurts me. I know I'll try."

They both nodded and followed Sarah's lead. They talked about the present and the future alone. They chatted quietly for a while longer, then each of them held the baby, marveling at the blond hair she'd gotten from Scott, and at how perfectly each of her tiny features had been formed.

Finally, as it approached nine, Sarah

kissed Grace's forehead and left her baby in the care of the nurses for another night. She couldn't wait to have her home in her crib where the precious doll Kip had given her waited.

Her parents had intended to stay in the hotel across from CHOP but Sarah thought they needed time together. She talked them into staying at her apartment where she would sleep on the sofa and give them her bed.

She pulled into her parking spot in front of the carriage house and got out of the car. "This is home. I live over the garage. It started life as a carriage house. Kip's sister lives there," she said pointing at Miriam's house just as the redheaded tornado tore out her back door. "Miriam, I'd like you to meet my parents," Sarah called out.

Miriam spun around and stopped dead in her tracks. "Sarah! Oh, Sarah! Thank God you're here."

Miriam's distress sent fear spiraling through Sarah. "What's wrong?"

"Kip's secretary just called. He's in trouble."

Kip tried the landing gear one more time. The warning light stayed on. The gear hadn't locked. "Valley Green Tower, this is AA—8493 again. That is once again a negative on gear lock. I repeat that is a negative."

"Kip, it's Joy."

"Hey, partner," he said into the mouth-piece of his radio. "I'm afraid today may be my day to bend up the equipment a little." He tried to sound relaxed for the sake of his four passengers, but it was incredibly soothing to his fraying nerves to hear her familiar voice at that moment. The only voice he'd rather hear was Sarah's but he wouldn't want her to be as worried as he was.

"That's what insurance is all about, Kip," Joy said. "Just so you don't bend you or your passengers. I've talked this over with our ground crew and the crews from a few other airlines. We have two ways to handle this. Can you divert to Wilmington or Philly International?"

Could he? He looked at his fuel gauge and did a quick calculation on his fuel, the wind speed and his air time. "It's a possibility. Close, but I'm not sure either is doable. It'd only work if the landing gear will come back up. The drag of the gear is using up fuel and fast."

He tried to retract it. Waited. Nothing.

"That's a negative. Gear will not retract either. Give me a minute. Let's see if I can manually get it back up or force it to lock."

He flicked on the auto pilot and rushed to the panel in the floor just outside the cockpit where the hand crank was located above the front wheel. He tied a rope around his waist then around one of the passenger seat bases. Air rushed into the compartment when he popped open the access panel.

The twinkling lights of the houses below caught his attention. They were dizzying and beautiful at once as they rushed by below. He looked away and ripped the hand crank out of its bracket and fitted it into the gear assembly. Bracing himself, he tried to turn it but it was a no go. One of the passengers must have realized he couldn't budge it alone. He climbed into the compartment across from him.

"You should be tied off," Kip argued.

"Next time. Let's get this done."

Muscles bulging and straining with the effort, the two of them didn't move the crank even a fraction of an inch in either direction. Kip pretty quickly realized that something was just plain broken in the assembly. He shook his head and motioned the guy out of the compartment.

"What now?" the man asked as Kip replaced the cover and locked it back down.

All four men were staring at him expectantly. Hopefully. He didn't have much of an answer. "Now I figure out a way to get us down safely." He clapped the guy on the shoulder. "Thanks for trying. You could all pray. Get right with the Lord and ask His help. I can use all the guidance from above I can get right now."

He rushed forward and got back behind the yoke. "Valley Green Tower, this is AA-8493. That is a no go on Wilmington or Philly. The landing gear will *not* retract."

"Kip. It's still Joy here. You can't divert?"

"It's too close, partner. This drag could leave me short of the runway. There's just too much housing between here and both of them. It's too great a risk for people on the ground and us up here. And I'd rather go with a dry landing with no foam here where I'm at least sure I have a runway. I-95 is too crowded to use at this time of night if I come up short," he said flippantly. It was pilot humor at its worst but he wasn't feeling too jovial.

Not surprisingly neither was Joy. "It'll be okay, Kip. The gear may be fine. It could be locked and the warning light is the only error," Joy said encouragingly.

"Or not," he responded.

"Anything I can do besides pray?" she asked.

"You could tell that foam truck to step on it and spread it thick. I'll be on fumes by then." And fumes could be more dangerous than a loaded fuel tank. You just never knew.

"Already done," came Joy's clipped reply. "We're praying, partner."

"I guess I'd better get on that myself. And, in the meantime, I'll just be up here... circling."

When his radio went silent, prayer and eternity weren't what popped into his mind. His eternity had been assured since age ten when he answered an altar call at vacation Bible school. What burst into his mind now was his wasted life.

Here he was, possibly minutes from pancaking onto the airfield, and all he could think about was Sarah the last time he'd seen her.

She'd been so furious with him, and so hurt. But mad as she'd been, she'd still been fighting for the life she knew they could have together.

A life he'd denied her. Refused to take a chance on.

It would be funny if it wasn't so sad. He'd been so worried about dying in eight years, he'd never even thought about checking out sooner. Even after she'd mentioned the possibility that an accident could take her first, he'd been so wrapped up in the scenario he'd constructed surrounding his own death that he hadn't really thought about what she'd been saying. What she'd meant.

Anyone could go home to be with the Lord at any time.

Life held no guarantees. God was in control, not man.

Not him.

Kip banked into another turn, once again heading back toward Valley Green Field. He checked the fuel gauge and grimaced. It was going fast.

Just like his life had. There was an awful lot of living he hadn't done.

His radio squawked. The tower just checking to make sure he was still there. "Circling. Trying not to run out of fuel before you're ready." He assured them he was on another approach and signed off again, wishing the voice had been someone he knew well. Someone who really knew him.

But there weren't very many of those. He thought of all the people whose lives he'd touched. He knew the reason he'd always felt he was on the outside looking in at their lives. He'd never allowed most of them to touch him—not really. He'd always thought he was trying to protect them from grieving his loss too deeply.

But it hadn't been that at all.

He did things for others all the time but he never let anyone do anything for him in return. He hadn't even wanted their thanks. It hadn't been pride on his part, thank God. But it certainly wasn't that he'd been overly gallant either. He'd always thought their gratitude embarrassed him and that it was a question of it being his honor to serve.

It *was* that. He hadn't fooled himself to the extent that he hadn't known his own mind. But he had to admit it had also been his way of leaving the world in some way beholden to him. A way to mark his name on the hearts of those he left behind so they'd remember him in a positive way.

It had been a good life as he'd constructed it. Not perfect but good enough.

Until Sarah.

He'd been a fool. All his planning had been for nothing. He'd still be right where he was at that moment—in a busted plane, in danger of dying—even if his health was perfect and if his ancestors had lived into their eighties. People died young everyday.

He checked his fuel consumption again and adjusted his air speed a few knots. Then banked into another turn to approach the airfield. Maybe it would be over on this pass. He was getting antsy to just do it and live or die with the results. The waiting was killing him anyway! Slowly!

Kip took a deep breath trying to ready his mind, heart and soul for what lay ahead. *I'm so sorry, Lord,* he prayed silently. *It was all so out of my control. There I was, eighteen years old with life bursting with promise. And then...* Kip shook his head. The Lord knew better than he did what he'd felt that day his aunt had redirected his future. *I guess I just decided to control what I could. But I can't, can I? If today's the day You call me, I'm gone. I won't have a choice. Now there's a lesson learned too late. I should have listened to Sarah. Now, if I don't get us out of this, she'll never know how much I wanted a life with her and Grace.*

I'm sorry. If You could give me a little extra skill and get me out of this, I'd sure be grateful. I'm not trying to bargain, but if I do get out of this alive, I'm going to ask Sarah to marry me. And I'm going to grab every second of every day You'll give me. I'll make it enough. I'll make it worth the pain she'll feel when I'm gone. I'll make her feel so loved while I'm here it'll make up for all the lonely years before she met me and the ones after I'm gone.

His starboard engine coughed, grabbing Kip's attention. Then it caught. "Valley Green Tower, this is AA-8493. What's the ETA on that truck? I'm about out of fuel and two minutes out. I need that runway. Now."

"AA-8493, your partner is helping the foaming operation. And we're working on some extra lighting. We're all but ready for you. As soon as you're lined up with runway one-niner, start your approach. We're lighting 'er up now."

Kip took a deep breath and called back to his passengers, "Assume crash positions, guys. And, hey, I got an A in crash landing in flight school so relax. We're going to be fine."

He had just lined up for his final approach

when both engines coughed and this time went silent. "Valley Green Tower. AA-8493 is lined up on approach—coming in dead stick."

Suddenly the runway lit up brighter than it ever had on a night approach. Then he realized cars had lined up along the top end of the runway. Their headlights shone on a runway bright white and thick with foam. He'd never seen a more welcome sight.

Kip glided her in and set her down as easily and slowly as he could. The gear touched the runway. He used the flaps to slow their forward motion even more. The gear held for another second or two as they passed the last car. Then just when he thought he had total control of the landing, the nose slammed forward into the ground as the front gear folded. Then the aft gear collapsed and the tail skidded left. And then the plane was pinwheeling out of control.

Just like life.

If he'd ever seen a more appropriate metaphor, he didn't know what it could be. He braced himself against the now worthless yoke. "It's all You, Lord," he said and readied himself for whatever lay ahead. It was out of his hands. Apparently it had never really been up to him at all.

Chapter Sixteen

The plane spun like an out-of-control carousel for hundreds of yards down the runway, foam spewing everywhere. The sound of steel tearing and crushing beneath the weight of the plane was something that Sarah knew would live in her nightmares for years. There was a loud gasp from the assembled spectators as the plane left the runway on the far side of the field. The nose caught in the dirt and burrowed into the turf. Then the tail rose in the air till the craft stood on end. Then, mercifully, rather than flipping forward onto its roof, the stiff wind caught the crippled plane and knocked it backward and sideways. The wing ripped off but then it dropped back to earth to settle on its belly. Then the beast, its rampage over, lay spent and silent.

The racket left in its wake a heavy silence that seemed to descend over the small airfield as they all held their breath waiting for something. Then before Sarah could ask what it was they thought might happen the wait was over.

A fire truck shot forward across the grassy field and the din of three ambulances and several pickup trucks revving their engines filled the air. Then they too tore off toward the mutilated aircraft, following the fire truck in a new flurry of urgent activity.

Sarah started running then, heedless of her parents and Miriam calling after her that it might be dangerous. No matter. She couldn't stop. Regardless of the danger, she had to see with her own eyes if Kip was all right. After she saw him, she wasn't sure what she'd do. She just knew she had to see him and make sure he was okay. He'd been in the nose of that plane when it stood on end. The nose that was now crushed into a wrinkled tangle of steel.

The smell of chemicals in the foam permeated the air but didn't quite overpower the odor of burnt rubber and overheated steel. Also in the air was urgency.

The ground crew was already trying frantically to pry the hatch open. They were getting nowhere because the bottom of the big steel door was crushed and torn into a mass of fused metal. The firefighters from the fire engine sprayed some more foam, onto the engines this time, she supposed as a precaution. Then two men ran to the plane with the hydraulic tool usually called the jaws of life.

They pushed it between the hatch and the fuselage and started it up. The hatch groaned a minute later and a loud crack echoed across the airfield. It had finally given way. Everyone seemed to breath a sigh of relief as someone in a uniform hopped up into the plane. Then a man quickly emerged from the yawning darkness of the fuselage.

But it wasn't Kip. This man was dark-haired and he wore a wool suit jacket. A passenger. Sarah stood on tiptoe but couldn't see past the dozen or so tall rescue workers who crowded near the opening. Moving left then right, trying to get to the plane, Sarah wove her way through the would-be rescuers, stepping over hoses and discarded tools of their trade. She was dimly aware that it was cold and that the foam was beginning to soak through her shoes, but she paid no attention to physical discomfort. Where was Kip?

One after another, the rest of the passengers emerged and were led and helped toward the paramedic trucks and ambulances. But still no Kip.

Then the crowd parted a little and she spotted Joy talking to someone who'd crouched down next to the plane. It was Kip, his blond hair blowing in the breeze the way it had the day she met him. He looked hale and hearty as he examined the plane's crushed underbelly with his partner. Then he stood and laughed at something someone said. He turned toward the hatch and spoke to a paramedic, who jumped to the ground and pulled his big kit out behind him. Kip must have cracked a joke because several of the men laughed as did the medic.

Sarah felt a blush heat her face as a path between them opened up further. She shouldn't be there. What was she doing? She took a step back, suddenly embarrassed. He'd made it quite plain he didn't want her around. But before she could pivot and slink away, Kip, as if drawn by some invisible force, turned sharply. His gaze locked with hers across the space separating them.

Never taking his eyes off Sarah, Kip said something to Joy, handed her a clipboard, then loped across the expanse between them. When he reached Sarah, he stopped, pausing a few feet away. "How did you know?"

"Miriam. She was on her way here when I got home. I had to come. I'm sorry if I made this whole thing more difficult for you but I had to know you were okay."

"No. Stop. There's no one I'd rather find waiting." Then the space between them seemed to disappear and she found herself in his arms held so tightly she could hardly breathe. But that was just fine. She didn't need all that much air as long as Kip was holding her and the air she breathed was full of the special scent of lime and leather and Kip. She grabbed a fistfull of his jacket and held him as tightly as he held her.

Nothing had ever felt so good as that soul-deep hug. It was an affirmation that he was alive. They just stood there with everyone milling around them until someone bumped into her. It seemed to bring Kip to an awareness of where they were. He let go of her and took her hand, looking around. "Come on. Over here," he said and pulled her to stand in front of the fire truck where they'd be out of the path of all the activity. The heat of the engine warmed the frigid air, too. Only then did she realize how awfully cold it was.

He cupped her face and kissed her sweetly then pulled her close in his arms again. His scent enveloped her again and chased away all the scary smells that reminded her of how close a call he'd had.

"When I was up there just circling, you were all I could think about, Sarah," he said next to her ear. "You and the opportunity to be happy with you that I nearly threw away. I was so sure I could control what future I had left but I could have died right here. Tonight. That's what you were trying to tell me. Any of us can go at any time."

Sarah couldn't find her voice. She just nodded against his chest then tipped her head back to stare up at him. And then he dipped his head and covered her waiting lips with his.

"I love you," he told her when he broke the kiss, breathing the words against her lips.

"I love you, too," she whispered back. "So much. I didn't know what love felt like until you."

"I didn't either. I called my mom last week. I asked her about my dad the way you suggested. She was pretty horrified that I thought she might have regretted marrying him because of the grief she suffered later. But even so, I still couldn't get past knowing I'd eventually hurt you that same way."

"Kip, I told you—"

"Shhh. And now I understand. There aren't any guarantees. I made myself and God a promise up there while I was circling I mean to keep. So," he took half a step back, took hold of her hand. Before she understood his intention, still holding her hand, he grinned and dropped to one knee in the torn-up, foamy and frozen grass. He looked up at her, his eyes shining with love and his blond hair glimmering in the light of the fire truck's headlamps. "Sarah Bates, will you do me the very great honor of becoming my wife?"

Sarah suddenly became aware of silence all around. She cut her gaze to the side. "Uh, Kip, we have a rather large audience."

He grinned and shrugged but looked only at her. "Then tell me yes. They probably all think a smart, talented woman like you would be nuts to get hitched to a loser fly-boy who just crashed a million dollars' worth of aircraft."

The audience had already faded into

meaninglessness. "Then they'd be wrong. Nothing would make me happier than to marry you."

Kip jumped up, scooped her into his arms and spun her around, laughing. Their audience burst into applause. He set her down and kissed her again. "I have to talk to some people. Would you mind staying with me? I'll drive you home and we can make some plans. Okay?"

She gave him a cheeky grin, feeling more confident of her place in his life. "Just try getting rid of me. But first I need to thank you. My parents came, Kip. They told me you wrote them about the way they've treated me. They're sorry. I really think they're sorry."

He cupped her face again and kissed her nose. "I couldn't stand by and watch them hurt you with their neglect any longer. You were so alone and I knew I was only hurting you by stepping in when you needed support. I couldn't stay away knowing you needed someone there with you either. Contacting them seemed like the only solution."

She tiptoed and kissed his cheek. "I know why you did it. Thank you. I love you for being you. So, what do you need to do first?"

He turned toward the wreckage. "Well, I

have to get checked out by the paramedics. I promised them a shot at me even though I know I'm fine. And I need to talk to the feds. It's their job to investigate. I think I'd rather get that over with first. And, then—" he stopped talking and staggered a little to the side. He shook his head.

"Kip, what is it?"

"Just a little dizzy. That was quite a carnival ride. But I'm sure I didn't hit my head or anything like that, not even when we stood on end. I'm fine."

They walked toward the wreckage hand in hand. There were three men standing with Joy obviously waiting for Kip. They wore navy-blue jackets and held clipboards. "Congratulations," Joy said when they got to the plane.

Close up the wreckage looked more mangled than she'd even thought. Big portable floodlights now ringed the aircraft turning night into day.

"You still have my flight log?" Kip asked Joy. When she handed it to him, he looked it over again, then gave it to one of the investigators. Sarah stood with Kip, listening to his explanation of what had gone wrong. He went into such exacting detail she marveled that he could have kept so clear a head when his life and the lives of his passengers had hung on his every decision.

He'd been talking to the federal investigators for about ten minutes when she noticed Kip growing a little restless. He seemed distracted, too, even though he continued to respond to questions. His answers, however, began to lack the precision they'd had minutes before.

Then he put his hand to his chest, frowning. He shifted to the side and put his arm around her shoulders. But not for closeness or for emotional support. She realized that what he sought was physical support. His weight shifted onto her even more. Sarah looked up at him and even in the light of the spotlights she thought he looked pale. "Kip. Are you okay?" she asked, interrupting the investigator.

Kip looked down at her and blinked as if trying to clear his vision. "Sarah?" he asked slowly and his knees buckled.

Then Joy was there, making a grab for him or he would have pulled Sarah to the ground with him. The two of them with the help of one of the federal officials managed to lower him to the ground. The paramedics charged over then and muscled Sarah aside.

Joy clasped hands with Sarah and it was impossible to tell who was squeezing the other's hand harder. She started praying even though she felt as if her world had just imploded. Because of that really. Her prayer was simple because her emotions and thoughts were in such a turmoil. "Please. Please. Please," she prayed, trusting that God knew her need. She needed Kip and the life they had only just promised each other.

Then the paramedic with the stethoscope confirmed her worst fear. "I don't have a heartbeat," the man told his partner.

"He's barely got a pulse. We're losing him!" the other confirmed.

"Grab the defibrillator. I think he's in v-tac or some other kind of arrhythmia," the first medic shouted as he fisted his hands together and started doing chest compressions. "Come on Kip! Breathe! Does anyone know if he has a history of arrhythmia?" he asked.

Sarah could barely breathe. She felt numb as she watched them cut through his shirt after stripping him out of his jacket. She picked it up off the ground and hugged it. It smelled like him. Leather and lime.

"His father died of some sort of heart

problem he says no one could ever diagnose. So did his uncle," Joy said.

Miriam came running up then and just stood wide-eyed, staring in horror. "This can't be happening! Not now."

"Clear," the medic not doing CPR shouted. The other one quickly sat back.

Kip's whole body jumped. But then he went still as death again. The medic twisted a dial and repeated the exercise with the same terrible lack of results. Then he turned the dial again. This time, though, the one with the stethoscope smiled when he listened to Kip's heart. "Sinus rhythm. He's back."

With that Kip's eyelids fluttered, then he opened them. "What?" he asked, clearly confused. "What happened?" he demanded, his mind growing more alert. Then he tried to push himself up into a sitting position.

The paramedic pushed him back to the ground. "Whoa! You aren't going anywhere but to a hospital."

"Paoli Memorial, don't you think?" the paramedic who'd been using the defibrillator asked the other. "It's a great heart hospital, Kip. They'll fix you right up."

An ambulance crew pulled a stretcher next

to him then and Kip looked a little frantic. He cast his gaze about at everyone standing around him until he found her and visibly relaxed. "Sarah?"

The question in his voice could have been asking any number of questions but the answer to every one of them was still the same. She nodded. "I'm coming, too. You aren't getting rid of me that easy, mister. I have lots of witnesses to that marriage proposal."

"I'll follow with your parents, Sarah," Miriam told her while they lifted him on the stretcher.

"You didn't want to ride with him, did you?" Sarah asked his sister.

"Yes, but you belong with him. I'm just his big sister. Take good care of my little brother. I'll call Mom and the others. And Sarah. *This is a blessing.* Kip just got a second chance. I'm sure of it."

Sarah couldn't understand why Miriam thought Kip having what looked like a massive heart attack at age thirty-two was a blessing. But all the way to the hospital as she sat in front next to the driver she prayed things weren't as bad as they seemed. Kip kept craning his neck so he could see her and she kept smiling and telling him he'd be fine. But, Miriam's strange statement notwithstanding, Sarah didn't see how.

Chapter Seventeen

Sarah hopped down out of the ambulance to meet Kip as they unloaded him. She looked up at the hospital. It wasn't as large as the Hospital of the University of Pennsylvania that sat next to CHOP but the ambulance driver told her it was a premier heart hospital of the region.

Kip reached for her hand as they pulled the gurney out of the ambulance. "I'm sorry, Sarah. I thought we'd get some time together. I wasted what little we had."

"Kip, stop. They're going to help you."

Looking sad, he shook his head. "There's something wrong. I feel really weak and my heart feels weird. I think I'm dying, Sarah."

"Kip, don't talk that way," she said and prayed she was right. Still holding his hand,

Sarah walked beside the gurney, listening with half an ear as the paramedics gave their report to a doctor who met them as they continued to roll him into the emergency ward.

Sarah looked back at Kip when his hand went limp in hers. "Kip!" she shouted, drawing the attention of the paramedics and the young woman doctor. She put a stethoscope to his chest and frowned. "Code Blue. Let's move, guys. Get him into Bay Two. The crash cart's already in there. Page Doctor Muller," she told a nurse as they rushed past.

Sarah tried to follow but the nurse stepped in the way. "You don't want to be in there. I know you think you do but you need to let them do their thing." The nurse grabbed a phone that hung outside the cubicle and paged Doctor Muller as ordered.

Sarah stood in the hall staring at the door, praying that once again they'd get his heart started. But she also recognized that his heart could only sustain just so much damage. She loved Kip too much to want him to live as a cardiac cripple, grounded and unable to soar in the sky the way he loved.

It was the hardest prayer she had ever prayed but she put her hand on the closed door and whispered brokenly, "Your will, Lord. Not mine."

She stood there, praying with her hand on the door for what felt like an hour but was probably more like ten minutes. Then finally the door swung open and Sarah stepped back as the doctor emerged.

"We've got him stabilized," she said and put her hand out to shake Sarah's hand. "I'm Doctor Michelle Kane. Try to relax. I've called in the biggest guy in the area in the field of cardiac intervention. If anyone can help your husband, it's him."

"Fiancé," Sarah explained and felt a tear roll onto her cheek, as she added, "for all of ten minutes." She dashed away the tears. "All the men in his family die young. He thought he had a few more years," she said.

The doctor looked sharply at her. "Wait a minute. All?" She motioned with her hands, encouraging Sarah to add more. "Come on. Tell me everything you know."

"You think it could be important?"

"If I've learned one thing working with Doctor Muller, it's that the most insignificant information can solve a mystery and we have a whopper here with your Kip."

Sarah was surprised the doctor found heart

attacks a mystery even as young as Kip was. It was unusual but not unheard of. "I don't understand. What's mysterious about a heart attack?"

"I don't know for sure but the complete absence of pain indicates this *isn't* a heart attack. We've already drawn blood to check for enzymes but dollars to donuts it'll come up negative. And I have a tech doing an ultrasound of the heart right now. I'm hoping it'll show no damage."

Hope surging through her, Sarah tried to remember everything either Kip or Miriam had told her about the history. "Okay, Kip tried to find out what might be wrong but the doctors he saw never found anything wrong in his tests. It really frustrated Kip because the same thing happened with his dad and uncle. Kip believes he'll die before he turns forty the way they did. It happened with his grandfather and great-grandfather, too. Both his father and uncle saw doctors who said they were fine. His uncle saw one in the morning and was dead before the afternoon was over. Kip's sister said their father was in bed and when they went to wake him in the morning he was dead. His uncle seemed to have laid down for a nap on the sofa. She said their autopsies were inconclusive—whatever that means."

Doctor Kane nodded. "He's being monitored right now and that may confirm what I'm starting to think is going on." She took Sarah's hand and squeezed it. "If you're a praying woman, pray that I'm right.

"Why don't you go clean up those tear stains. I have a call to make to Doctor Muller. Then we'll go in and see Kip together. We'll probably be taking him off for some tests and such after that."

Sarah nodded, rushed into the ladies' room, washed her face and tried to cover the ravages of her tears with cool water. After running a comb through her hair she tore back out.

Doctor Kane hung the phone on the cradle, closed a folder she hadn't had before and turned toward her as she approached. "Ready?" she asked.

"As I'll ever be," Sarah said. "Has anyone told his sister anything?"

Doctor Kane nodded. "I sent word out to them that he's stable. Let's go."

Sarah took a deep breath, plastered a big smile on her face and followed Doctor Kane into the small room. Kip was sitting up in bed wearing a hospital gown and over his head was a flat-screen monitor showing heart rate, blood pressure and a variety of other wavy lines running across the surface. "You look better," she told him.

"Hey," he said and she could tell he was trying for a light tone. "If things keep going this way, we may set a record for the shortest engagement in history. The Lord keeps trying to take me and these guys keep dragging me on back."

Sarah felt her smile waver but she kept it in place as best she could. "That's probably because I told them I've only just wangled a proposal out of you and I want my happily ever after. You're not getting away this easily."

Doctor Kane spoke up then. "We're not giving up, Kip. Don't you," she ordered. "Just in case I'm right about what I think may be wrong with you, I've given you a medication that will hopefully stave off another episode."

The door opened again and a tall balding man in a long white lab coat with glasses perched on the edge of his nose bustled into the room. "Is this the mystery man I'm hearing so much about?" he asked.

Kip put his hand out and the doctor shook

it, introducing himself as Doctor Winton
Muller. Doctor Kane introduced Sarah as
Kip's fiancé and he shook her hand and told
her not to look so worried. Then he picked
up an EKG printout and pointed something
out to Doctor Kane who smiled and nodded.
Then Muller looked up with a wide smile.

"Kip Webster, you have no idea what a
lucky young man you are. This brilliant
young woman is a student of mine. She just
happened to be passing through the E.R. as
the paramedics radioed that they were
bringing you in. It looks to me as if she may
have neatly solved the mystery I hear is in
your family."

"There's no mystery except why we die.
We still do."

Muller pulled a rolling food tray over to
the bed and laid the EKG printout on it. He
pointed to an irregular line at the bottom.

Sarah stepped closer to the bed to see what
it was the doctor was pointing out and Kip
took her hand, holding tightly. She looked at
him, then pushed a stray lock of his hair off
his forehead before she glanced down at the
paper the doctor had spread out.

"This is an indication of an extra electrical
pathway running between the upper and

lower chamber of your heart." Doctor Muller said. "It's called a Wolff-Parkinson-White pathway. In your case, I imagine you've inherited the tendency considering the family history your fiancé gave Doctor Kane. In most folks who have this it's not dangerous or even all that bothersome. For a very few— you and I'm thinking your ancestors—it can be deadly.

"What it usually causes is a fast heart rate. In you, it's causing a severely abnormal heart rhythm that then caused a cessation of blood flow from your heart to your body. Basically it's causing your heart to short circuit."

"Doctor Kane said she put me on a medication. Will that cure it or stop it?" Kip asked, sounding hopeful again at last.

"It could help but I have to tell you it's a tough medication on the body and it might not be all that reliable a treatment in the long run."

Kip's shoulders slumped and he expelled a disappointed sounding breath. "Then there's nothing surefire?" he asked.

The doctor grinned. "Son, it's moments like this that I live for. We have a procedure that doesn't just treat it. It's almost always a complete cure. What I'll do is thread a catheter through your blood vessels into your inner heart. There will be an electrode at the end of the catheter that I'll heat and ablate—that's destroy—a small spot of heart tissue. That will block the extra pathway. It's relatively low risk and highly effective."

"So, when would you do this?" Kip asked; his tone spoke primarily of confusion.

Both doctors looked at each other, then Muller checked his watch. "You have anything penciled in at midnight?"

"You would do it that soon?" Sarah asked.

Kip smiled a little sadly and squeezed her hand. "I think what the doctor means, sweetheart, is he'd better fix it now before my heart stops again."

"Oh." Sarah's heart fell as she nodded. Did that mean they might be out of time together?

"We'll take you up in a few minutes. You two visit while we go check to make sure the cath lab is all set for us. I'll see you up there. Your fiancé can wait in the green room just down the hall from the lab. Any other family members can wait there with you. Try not to worry. Cardiac caths are extremely routine and this is just a minor change to that routine."

Sarah felt a smile bloom on her face. He smiled benignly, then nodded to Doctor

Kane and left, his long coat once more flapping behind him.

"Someone will be in to have you sign off on the procedure," Doctor Kane said then.

"Thank you, Doctor. If you hadn't passed through the E.R. when you did…" Kip said.

"But I did. Sometimes things just happen the way they're supposed to," Dr. Kane said and then she was gone too.

And they were alone.

Kip stared at the closed door. He looked dumbstruck. "That's…that's it?" he asked, disbelief in his tone.

"I know. I don't think I've ever had such good news seem so impossible."

"He seemed to know what he's talking about," Kip said, sounding a touch more hopeful.

Sarah smiled. "Dr. Kane told me Muller is the leading cardiologist in the region and he specializes in cardiac intervention. I take it to mean he steps in and prevents damage rather than dealing with what happens after damage occurs. Yes, I'd say he knows what he's talking about."

"I want to believe it. But this has been hanging over my head for so long…it's a lot to absorb. You know?"

She nodded.

Kip sat there thinking, staring down at their clasped hands for a few minutes. Then he looked up, smiling broadly. "This isn't going to kill me. Sarah, we have a real chance to have it all!"

Sarah smiled, then tears welled up in her eyes. "Honestly, I've turned into a garden sprinkler! And Miriam's going to be unbearable after this," she sniffled. "The last thing she said to me was that this was going to be a second chance for you. I couldn't imagine a heart attack being a blessing but that's what she said. And she was right. Because it wasn't a heart attack at all. Oh, Kip if you hadn't crashed, the paramedics wouldn't have been there. If your landing gear hadn't malfunctioned, you'd have landed and gone home. You'd have fallen asleep," her voice caught.

"And never woken up—just like my dad and Uncle Galen." He pulled her into his arms and hugged her tight. "Thank you, Lord. Thank you. Thank you. Thank you."

Epilogue

On a day that Kip had never hoped to enjoy, he waited at the end of the Tabernacle's middle aisle for Sarah.

For his June bride.

And she'd be on her father's arm. Sarah's relationship with her parents had strengthened over the last months. Tentative though the connection had been at first, each time Adam and Theresa stepped up to the plate and didn't disappoint her or Grace, Sarah's trust in them grew.

Grace had come home in time for Easter, still undersized and on oxygen but bright, happy and raring to go. She already called him Da-da. Only one sound was more precious to his way of thinking and that was the sound of "I love you" on Sarah's lips.

As sure as he was that this marriage was made in heaven, Kip had insisted on a six-month engagement. He refused to rush her to the altar as her first husband had done. Sarah had agreed that though they were sure of their love it had all happened rather quickly. As far as Kip was concerned it had been a courtship made in heaven as well. There seemed to be nothing they didn't agree on now that they'd solved the cause of the one and only fight they'd ever had. The one in the coaching office at the school.

The keyboard player changed tunes then, and Miriam and Joy appeared at the end of the aisle to walk forward together. They both wore what Sarah had called basic black cocktail dresses. He knew they were an odd set of witnesses but regardless of convention, his partner was his best friend and his sister had all but adopted his future wife. They beamed their love and support to him, and his love for them made his eyes to mist over.

Sometimes he still couldn't believe that the shadow of impending death had been lifted from his life. But he was confident it had been. His heart was fine. The extra pathway had been blocked. The surgery had been a complete success. He and Sarah had a long and happy future ahead. He just knew it.

Sarah and her father came into view then and as planned, she carried Grace in her arms. Her mother had made their coordinating dresses so he'd seen a piece of the pale blue silk and the soft white lace that flowed over it. But the sneak peek hadn't prepared him for Sarah in the finished product.

She nearly stole his breath in the floor-length dress that showed off her small waist and her slender arms with its short cap sleeves. Matching blue satin ribbons and tiny satin roses were woven through her shiny chestnut tresses. Around her neck and at her ears she wore the pearls his grandfather had brought back from China after World War II. His mother had passed them on to Sarah—the wife of one fly-boy to another then another.

"Da-da!" Grace shouted, as she pulled off the headband that matched the ribbons and flowers in Sarah's hair. He chuckled as his new daughter held out her arms to him, waving her headband like a flag, leaning forward out of Sarah's arms. She squirmed so much Sarah was clearly having a problem holding on to her in the slippery lacy dress that was so much like her mother's.

Kip rushed forward and met them halfway as Grace dove into his arms. He laughed as did Sarah, Adam and the rest of those attending. He couldn't love his new daughter any more if she was his biological child but he couldn't take his eyes off Sarah. There'd be time for Grace later.

"Who gives this woman?" Jim Dillon asked, starting a ceremony full of love, laughter and a few tears. With God's blessing, the life he and Sarah had ahead of them would be a lot like their wedding.

* * * * *

Dear Reader,

This was a very emotional and personal book for me. Twenty years ago, when the field of neonatology was young, my niece was born a day short of her twenty-third week of gestation. There seemed to be no hope, and doctors thought there was no way she would be born alive. They had no intention of trying to save her. Little Kelly had other ideas. At only one pound three ounces, she was all fight. She fought for breath and gave the astounded doctors no choice but to reward her fighting spirit by taking an unheard-of chance. Eleven and a half months later, Kelly made the six-o'clock news when she came home. She wore Cabbage Patch preemie clothes because there were no baby clothes small enough for her. Her road hadn't been easy and wouldn't be for some time. But "quit" was never in her vocabulary. She is the living embodiment that proves nothing is impossible for the Lord.

In *Time for Grace,* Kip travels his life alone by choice, and Sarah, who wants a family, seems destined to be alone. Kip too easily accepts his fate, and Sarah rages against it. They both had a lot to learn. But don't we all?

It is perhaps the most difficult lesson we learn, this leaning on God and trusting him and his secret plans for our lives. We forget that He can do anything. All we need is to have faith. So on days when going forward seems overwhelming, we should all remember Grace, who is the fictional account of our Kelly with all her one pound three ounces of fight. If she could set medical records just so she could have a shot at life, anything is possible for the rest of us. And if God is in our corner, He'll do more than half the work. We just have to believe.

Kate Welsh

QUESTIONS FOR DISCUSSION

1. Sarah struggled to understand why God let certain things happen to her. What were they, and why do you think God allows difficult circumstances in the lives of His people?

2. How did Sarah's anger at God hold her back in life? In her relationships?

3. Sarah felt guilty for resenting her parents and for her anger at God. How was she finally able to let that go?

4. How did Sarah's anger at God make her life harder? Why doesn't God want us to feel such crippling guilt as Sarah felt? How is it contrary to God's plan for us to hold on to guilt? What is the danger of holding on to guilt?

5. Kip prayed for God to send someone into Sarah's life, and it clearly turned out to be him, yet he resisted. When Sarah married Scott, she had doubts but let him

persuade her. How can we know if a circumstance comes from God or from our own desires? Does God always choose the hardest course for us or does it just seem that way since we don't know where the easier path will lead?

6. Was Miriam wrong to throw Kip and Sarah together? It turned out to be what God wanted for them, but was Miriam working from her own wishes for her brother's happiness, following the leading of the Lord, or did her interference get in the way of what God wanted? How was she wrong when it all turned out the way she thought it should?

7. There are several times during the book when Sarah thought God was punishing her for her anger and lack of faith. If God is all good, would He punish us here on earth? Or does He use tragedies, accidents and illness to lead us back to Him? There is little chance that Sarah would have met Kip had Grace not been born so prematurely. Does He use bad events for good, as He seems to have with Grace's birth?

8. Kip's faith was strong, but did he put his faith in God as far as his life and death were concerned?

9. Do you think God intervenes in our lives? Do you think He intervened with the near plane crash to make Kip see his mistake and to ultimately prolong Kip's life?

10. How did Kip's upbringing show itself in the way he chose to live his life? And how did the way Sarah grew up show in the things she wanted from life?

11. How much were Sarah and Kip affected by trying to keep control over their lives?

Love Inspired® SUSPENSE

RIVETING INSPIRATIONAL ROMANCE

Watch for our new series of
edge-of-your-seat suspense novels.
These contemporary tales
of intrigue and romance
feature Christian characters
facing challenges to their faith...
and their lives!

Steeple
Hill®

Visit:
www.SteepleHill.com

HISTORICAL

INSPIRATIONAL HISTORICAL ROMANCE

Engaging stories of romance,
adventure and faith,
these novels are set in
various historical periods
from biblical times
to World War II.

NOW AVAILABLE!

Steeple
Hill®

For exciting stories that reflect traditional values,
visit:
www.SteepleHill.com